The Tears That Flow Into The
KANAWHA RIVER

The Tears That Flow Into The
KANAWHA RIVER

Leon Breckenridge

XULON PRESS

Xulon Press
2301 Lucien Way #415
Maitland, FL 32751
407.339.4217
www.xulonpress.com

© 2021 by Leon Breckenridge

All rights reserved solely by the author. The author guarantees all contents are original and do not infringe upon the legal rights of any other person or work. No part of this book may be reproduced in any form without the permission of the author. The views expressed in this book are not necessarily those of the publisher.

Printed in the United States of America.

Paperback ISBN-13: 978-1-66281-316-0
Ebook ISBN-13: 978-1-66281-317-7

Dedication

Tears that flow into the Kanawha River and then flow into the Chicago River.

I WILL GET DOWN ON TWO KNEES IF THEY STOP THE BLACK-on-black killings in Chicago that are still happening today, even to innocent bystanders, including children such as the ones recently gunned down on July 4, 2020. Moments of silence for seven-year-old Natalie Wallace, three-year-old Mekhi James Jr., thirteen-year-old Amaria Jones, ten-year-old Lena Nunez, and one-year-old Sincere Graston. Also, a moment of silence for my best friend, Billy Thomas, who was an innocent bystander sitting on his porch drinking a glass of lemonade and was shot to death in Chicago.

I dedicate this book to the people that were buried in the African American cemetery because their remains were removed and put into one mass grave at the Meadow Haven Cemetery, just so the state could build a ramp for the Montgomery Bridge. I feel for these people and their families because their loved ones were disturbed. The African American cemetery was there since the late 1800s. A lot of these graves did not have headstones or markers on the graves. I remember the time Mrs. Lee, my neighbor, asked me to get a rock and place it on her mother's grave because she could not afford a headstone. There were a few graves left behind, which I do not believe is right. Just because they were at the top of the hill and out of the way of the state's construction, they did not think it was necessary to move them with the others.

I also dedicate this book to the following people who were a big part of my life growing up. Hazel and her husband, Paul Bego. Hazel was like my big sister. She was the one who talked me out of going into the Marines because of the Vietnam War. She said I would probably be killed. Hazel's husband, Paul, was like a brother to me, and he was genuinely nice to me. I respected Roger Castle, my old baseball coach who was a marine and a helicopter gunner. Roger was shot down and killed on his second trip to Vietnam.

I have much love and respect for Mrs. Pearl Price, who was a second mother to me. She taught me religion and how to pray. I will never forget when my mother left, and Mrs. Price said to me, "Remember your mother will always be your mother and you should always take care of her." Mrs. Bertha Washington was also like a mother to me. She lived above us and would watch us when my father went away. She taught English, drama, and French to the older children in high school. She was also one of the sponsors of the yearbook. Mrs. Washington produced a play called, "Raindrops" that I participated in when I was about eight years old. I played a raindrop and wore a raindrop costume.

I admired Mrs. Ida Wade, who was my primary school teacher at Simmons High School. She was strict and used corporal punishment on us, which was paddling us if we misbehaved. Mrs. Wade was an excellent teacher. She taught me how to do math well. Plus, she was a great mentor to me. She had a degree in education from West Virginia State College, and she graduated from the University of Atlanta and the University of Pittsburg.

I appreciated Mrs. Carter who mentored me and taught grade school; her husband was also a great mentor to me. They lived across the street from me and were great neighbors. Mrs. Carter had a Bachelor of Arts in Education from West Virginia State College. Mr. Carter was a deputy sheriff and worked at a state liquor store.

I was fortunate to know Mrs. Bertha Wood, who was another great mentor to me, but also another strict teacher. She taught well, and I thought she was smart. She majored in English and algebra, and she graduated from West Virginia State College. She was part of the "Y" teen club and a student counselor sponsor. I vividly remember when she died. I was only eleven years old, and I was one of her pallbearers.

Respect to Mr. James H. Martin, who was the father of my best friend, Alfred. Mr. Martin was killed while driving over the railroad tracks. He was a construction worker who helped build the Montgomery Bridge. His wake and funeral were held at the First Baptist Church as the first service in Montgomery, West Virginia, on January 24, 1956.

I dedicate this book to my father, Henry; my sister, Rose; my mother, Ethel, who passed away at ninety-one years old on March 7, 2016; and my younger brother, Roy L. Breckenridge, who died on March 13, 2020. Roy had just celebrated his seventieth birthday on February 7, 2020. He called me on his birthday to thank me for his birthday card. I sent him a Birthday Mass card that said, "As a spiritual gift, you have been enrolled in the Seraphic Mass Association and will share perpetually in Special Novenas of Masses celebrated throughout the year." I purchased the Mass card from a priest.

The overall creation of this book is dedicated to my family and friends that have made it possible to bring it to light. A special thank you to Julie M. Wesner for her assistance and Pauline Leslie for her insight.

All too often African Americans, black and brown people, are treated harshly and unjustly. I pray for justice for all of mankind and humanity. We are all Americans, and we just want to live a long life until we are old. "ALL LIVES MATTER."

Table of Contents

Chapter 1: Growing Up in West Virginia (1947–1967) 1
Chapter 2: Gossip and Mom Leaving 9
Chapter 3: Honoring My Father 15
Chapter 4: The Movement That Lead to Desegregation
in the Montgomery School System 21
Chapter 5: The Unexpected Journey 31
Chapter 6: The Witch City 39
Chapter 7: Post Office 45
Chapter 8: Retirement 57
Chapter 9: The Museum 63
Chapter 10: Memories 69

Chapter 1

Growing Up in West Virginia
(1947–1967)

I AM LEON BRECKENRIDGE. I WAS BORN IN MONTGOMERY, West Virginia, in 1947. I have a younger brother named Roy who was born in Montgomery in 1951. Montgomery, West Virginia, was known for its coal mining. The town was called the "Coal Valley Post Office" in the late 1800s. The town was small, having about twenty people, and it was highly segregated between the blacks and the whites. The blacks lived on one side and the whites lived on the other side, separated by the tracks. My mother stayed at home and was a homemaker. She was a beautiful woman of Afro and Cherokee descent. Her flowing silky black hair rested beyond her shoulders hugging her back. Her complexion glowed like caramel. My father, on the other hand, was an average-looking dark-skinned black man, who worked at the Atlantic and Pacific grocery store. My brother and I lived with our parents in a three-family home, in a five-room apartment. My brother and I shared a room and slept on bunkbeds. We were part of the African American community. We all lived close in a big community group that was surrounded by beautiful green lands and miles of woods, and I enjoyed spending time there.

There was a river nearby named "Kanawha," which is an Indian name. Some folks said Kanawha is a Shawnee word meaning water. Other folks say it's "Catawba," meaning friendly brother. Although I liked the name and meanings of this river, it was not the best-looking river because of the sewer drains. The nearby plants would release toxic material into it and it became contaminated and the air became polluted. This pollution affected the air quality of the African American community. Our only means of transportation was from the Montgomery train station. The two tracks nearby were for carrying coals and other materials. It was also used as a passenger train that traveled all over the country. My home was up on a hill from the river and the tracks. My brother and I were known as the "Hill Boys." Folks in the town started to call us that most likely because we lived up in the hills in the middle of nowhere. We didn't mind it at all and actually liked being called the Hill Boys. We had such a beautiful view from our home overlooking the city of Montgomery. Our distant neighbors probably envied us for having such view.

Though the winters were colder living near the river, I still found the beauty of living there. The snow and ice on the mountains were breathtaking. Even though my brother and I didn't spend much time together, I enjoyed sledding with him for hours with the other children. We couldn't afford a sled, so I borrowed one from one of my friends. We were a close community, and at nights we would build a bonfire to keep warm and socialize.

My mother, Ethel, got married to my father, Henry, at the age of 24. They celebrated their honeymoon at Fort Sam Houston, Texas. My father was an army medic. His last duty station was in Guam during World War II. One of my earliest and favorite memories of the holidays was Christmas with my mother, my father, and my brother and I together as a family. For Christmas my parents gave us an electric train set that I would watch for hours going around the track. It was a diesel Lionel model train that pulled the coal cars and caboose. It was black with a little bit of orange. As it went around, I enjoyed the strong smell of metal and oil burning. I could close my eyes and imagine it was a real train. I wouldn't leave the room for hours because I was so fascinated with it.

I remember being excited when my father bought us our first black-and-white television. The television brand was Zenith. It had a bulky bulb screen and was made out of mahogany wood. We were the first ones to have a television in our neighborhood. Every Saturday my grandmother, Mary-Lou, my aunts, my uncles, and my cousins would come over and enjoy watching TV with us because they didn't have one. One of my neighbors, Mrs. Pearl Price, loved coming over to watch western movies. She would watch my brother and me when my parents went away. I really liked it when she watched us because she was very nice, and she treated me like I was her son.

I remember going to grandma's house when I was between seven and nine years old. She lived about three miles from us, which wasn't too far, except for the mountains. Roy and I would walk there with Mom. It was a long walk down a rocky road in between the mountains. I often felt nervous because we had to cross a long, swinging rope bridge. It was made out of boards and rope, plus it was high above the rocky creek. I often worried it would collapse with us on there because the materials were not too strong. Even though I was nervous, I enjoyed the mountain view and the cool breeze coming from the water. When we arrived, Grandma would be waiting for us on her front porch, swinging calmly on her big wooden swing. She would rock back and forth as if she was in a rocking chair.

My grandmother lived there with my step-grandfather, Tom. I thought of him as my real grandfather because I grew up with him. They allowed my cousin, Paulette Herbert, to live there with them because she had nowhere to go. Grandma also took care of a little boy named Keith who had Down syndrome. She took him in because his parents didn't know how to take care of a disabled child. I think he was around the same age as Roy and me. I never treated Keith any different than I would treat my brother. I recalled my aunt Gertrude telling me the story about why my grandma left her previous husband. He abused her, and it got to the point of such physical abuse that it caused permanent injury to her body. He kicked her in her eye so hard it was damaged permanently, so it had to be removed. Nonetheless, I loved visiting my grandma. At times my mother, Roy, and I slept over, and it was fun. Unfortunately, she didn't have running water or a bathroom, so we had to use the outhouse. The outhouse was separate from the house and made out of wood. There was no handle to flush because it was just deep pit.

My grandmother had a small farm, and the family grew a lot of corn with some other vegetables. They had pigs, hogs, and chickens. I loved playing in the pigpen no matter how dirty and muddy it was. After I finished playing in the pigpen, I would get into a big steel tub to wash off. Grandma and Grandpa would get water from their well and heat it on the stove before they filled the tub for me. I looked forward to the morning because Grandma would get up at four in the morning and start cooking breakfast. She would prepare fresh buttered biscuits, fresh ham from the hog Grandpa killed, and fried chicken from the fresh chicken Grandma killed. She also made fresh eggs, home fries, and homemade jam. After breakfast we would all walk to the Donwood Baptist Church for worship and praise. Tom was the deacon at the church. It was such a long day of service, a good three hours of preaching from the minister and Tom. There was a lot of singing and dancing in between. After church we would go back to Grandma's house and have leftovers with some dessert. My favorite dessert was her sweet potato pie. Grandma always had plenty of desserts to choose from, like her butter cake and lemon meringue pie. After dessert we'd have to go back to church for about an hour. Church was more like an all-day service, and at times I was tired and wanted to sleep.

While I was at my grandma's, I enjoyed playing with Keith despite his disability. I played with him for hours at a time. He loved wrestling and playing tag with me. One day I visited my grandma, and I could not find Keith. It was then she told me that Keith had an accident and died. No one really knew how, but Keith somehow fell into the fireplace. That was one of the saddest moments of my life because I was close to him and loved playing with him. He was still a young boy about eight or nine years old at the time of his death.

After learning that Keith died, I began to reflect on what life was about because I was puzzled about death. As a young boy, whenever I saw a hearse carrying the dead, I ran quickly and hid because I wanted no part of it. Death to me was mystifying or something bad, and I could not see the good in it. I was young and naïve, and knew I feared dying. As I got older, I understood the life we live in our present moment in time could not be eternal. When I was perplexed about things, I would write a poem to reflect my thoughts because it brought healing and clarity. I wrote a poem about death because it allowed me to make sense of it.

LIFE'S MYSTERY

Wouldn't it be immense to live eternally?
I gravitate continuing to taste the wonders of life,
Shouldn't we all yearn to live forever internally?
But so, we breathe life so is death's rife,
Though some may suffer in the physical sense,
Countless would prefer this life over death,
To know the ending is near, the feeling is tense,
Couldn't we just shorten the days to life's length?
Illnesses be gone, and growing old no more,
The natural end of life, do we even have a choice?
Oh, the journey of life be this mystical folklore,
What is to celebrate the end of life, need no rejoice,
I believe God created the everlasting life spiritually,
If you believe in God you shall live everlasting,
As you grow older accepting death comes naturally,
No matter how we perceive living, life's enchanting.

By Leon Breckenridge

Leon Breckenridge as a baby

John Sturgeon and Henry Breckenridge

The 25th anniversary award of Produce Department Head Henry Breckenridge of Montgomery, W. Va., was presented by his manager, John Surgeon, and R. L. Wilson, his supervisor.

Henry's service with the company began August 22, 1942. He has gained experience in all departments and was recently promoted to produce department head.

He is a World War II Army veteran and resides at 209 Fayette Pike, Montgomery, **W. Va.**

Leon's father, Henry, around his retirement from the A&P grocery store

Leon's mother, Ethel

Leon's grandmother (Mary-Lou) and her husband, Tom

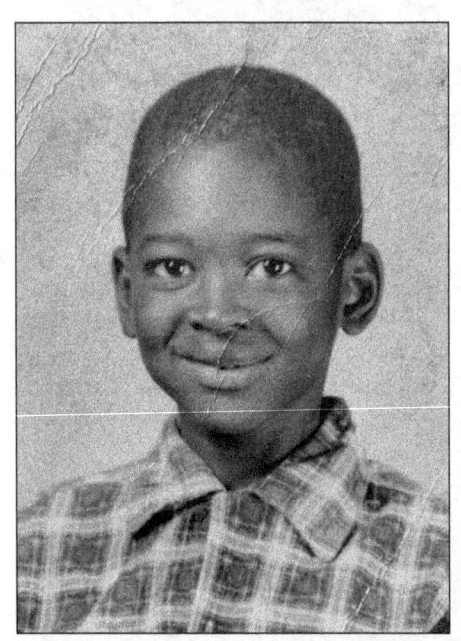

Leon's brother, Roy, at about age eight

Mrs. Pearl Price was a seamstress. She also loved to make quilts. Mrs. Price taught Roy and Leon about the Bible. She taught them how to pray before going to bed.

Chapter 2

Gossip and Mom Leaving

When I was about ten years old, things started to become a little hostile at home. I recall hearing the neighbors talking about my mother. I couldn't understand why because it didn't sound like my mom. I heard the same stories throughout the neighborhood about my mother. People were noticing that she was acting different. They said she seemed lost and confused as she would wander around town frequently. Some people were saying they thought she had a mental illness, like schizophrenia. My father noticed the difference in Mom but would not talk about it to us. The stories were getting worse, as we heard she was running around town naked. Some even saw her with other men, possibly even dating them. I was told one of them was my real father, and it really hurt me. I was upset and confused by all these stories spreading like wildfire about my mother.

One day I saw a little boy accidentally step on my mother's feet. I couldn't believe how my mother reacted. She struck him with her hand across his face really hard. It startled me to see my mother do that, and it made a great impact on me at that moment. The boy ran right home and got his mother, who then came down and screamed in my mother's face. She then walked away with the boy because she knew my mom had some kind of mental illness. It seemed as if Mom was getting worse. There was a time she randomly hit me on the shoulder with a broom handle so hard I fell to my knees and couldn't get up for a while because my whole body became numb. My mom went away for a while, and I was told she was institutionalized. My two aunts took care of my brother and me for about a month, so my father could continue to work.

Several months later, Mom came back home. I missed my mother, and I was eager to see her. I was looking forward to seeing her back to being Mom again, but I still didn't see her acting like the mom I knew. One day I was getting ready for school and it was raining so hard, Mom wanted me to cover my head so I wouldn't arrive at school soaked. I didn't own a hat, though. All of a sudden, Mom grabbed one of her scarfs and put it over my head. I started to cry because it was a woman's scarf, and I was embarrassed. I didn't want my classmates to see me like that because they would laugh and tease me all day. There I was wearing this bright pink-and-white girly scarf. I screamed and begged Mom to let me take it off. Miss Childs, one of my neighbors, heard me and yelled for me to come to her house. She then gave me a baseball cap. I was so relieved and loved this hat so much that I wore it all the time, to the point that it had obvious signs of wear and tear. It was a Brooklyn Dodgers hat, dark blue with a white letter "B" on it.

There were times when my mom would take me to wakes when someone she knew passed away. Wakes were held at family homes back then. I was scared because I didn't know what to expect. I remember one of the first times I attended a wake. It was for one of the coal miners who died in a freak accident. He was using the bathroom and a slate came down on his head. I remember going into the home and instantly noticing a strong odor. It was creepy because the lights were dimmed. I always stayed in the back while Mom went up to view the body. I was so glad that we left shortly after because I felt uncomfortable being around dead bodies.

One night when my dad wasn't home, I heard people talking quietly downstairs. I peeked down the stairway and saw Mom embracing and kissing another man. I recognized the man from the Montgomery Ice company. I was shocked but also sad and hurt seeing my mom with another man. Some nights Mom would force me to go out with her and one of her friends for a ride. I didn't know him, but I remember he was a tall man in an army uniform. We never went anywhere in particular. All we did was drive around town for hours. I was scared being in the car with him because he would speed and drive recklessly. Mom liked it, though, because she would laugh the whole time. Mom kept seeing other men, one after the other, for a few years. There was a time when I was a little bit older, in my early teens, I heard rumors that my mom was dating a police officer named Eddie Turner. People were saying that he was my real father. Even though it was upsetting and hurtful to hear, I wouldn't let myself believe that rumor. I was surprised to hear that it was Eddie Turner anyways, because I had known him for quite some time. I actually worked with him for a few years. He was a co-owner of a dry cleaners. We would drive around the Montgomery area to deliver the completed dry cleaning to his customers. Back then I would deliver the clothes to their homes and collect the money from them. I really liked him and his wife because they were very kind to me. Though I thought about the rumors at times, it was hard to believe because I bore no resemblance to him. And especially because I never saw my mother with him. My mom wasn't home much, and this made my dad suspicious about the men. I would hear my parents argue, and I recall one time that stuck out to me. My parents were arguing in their bedroom. I was nervous but curious to know what was going on. Their door was slightly cracked open, so I quickly walked up to the door and peeked in. I couldn't believe what I saw. My dad was holding a gun aimed right at my mother's body. It was a 12-gauge shotgun that he used to hunt squirrels. Mom was speechless and looked terrified as she just stood there. I looked on in such shock. I was so afraid for my mother and knew I could not do anything because I was helpless and scared.

Late one night about two weeks after the gun incident, I saw my mom packing a suitcase. This made me think she must have been talking to my aunt Gertrude or my grandma because she didn't have money to go anywhere. I didn't think Mom's mental health issues would allow her to think clearly enough to leave on her own. It was very quiet that night. You could hear a pin drop as my dad, my brother, Roy, and I looked on. I watched with such fear, worrying if I would ever see my mom again. I couldn't move a muscle. My body had this nervous and numb feeling, an empty, lonely feeling in my heart and mind. Mom never said a word. She walked right by us and downstairs with her suitcase in hand. Dad, Roy, and I walked down behind her. Mom quickly went right out the door. Still without a word, she walked down the hill, across the tracks, and right to the Montgomery train station. We weren't far behind, but we picked up our pace to catch up to her. There we were, the four of us just standing in silence. I knew it would be a while because it was 11:30 p.m. and the only train that came by was the Cardinal midnight train, every Wednesday night. It was a dark, warm summer night with a full harvest moon above, so close and bright it lit up the night. Other than us, just a couple other folks came by. I heard the hissing and screeching of the train getting closer and that familiar feeling of emptiness and loneliness went through my body. The train approached, and Mom stepped forward. The conductor opened and slid the metal door back as he called out, "All aboard." Mom gave Roy and me a quick kiss on the lips and just a wave goodbye to Dad before she walked up the steps of the train and vanished from our eyes. I was at a loss for words, hoping my dad or my brother would say something. But it was too late. The doors closed, and the train pulled away. I watched the train go around the mountains as it blew its whistle one more time.

 I longed for the return of my dear mother because life at home was never to be the same. It seemed that after Mom left, my father transitioned into someone else. He became unsympathetic, and the love he once had for my brother and me became distant. My father never told my brother and me that it was our fault that mom left, but the way he treated us was pure hatred and resentment. He behaved as if someone took a nail to his heart. Occasionally, I heard him whistle and hum to a collection of songs. One of his favorite songs was "Black Coffee" by Sarah Vaughan. He played the song, "I'm feelin' mighty lonesome" like a broken record. I never understood the song because I was a young boy, but it was a moment in my father's life where he found refuge and we found peace.

Goodbye, Mom

On a hot summer night, fireflies were lighting up the night. The nightingales were making their mating calls on the quietest night of all. As the summer mountain dew was quickly moving, things became gloomy. It was like watching a dark horror movie. As I felt the loneliness, my night became full of sadness. I knew love would never be the same as she walked away. As bad as I wanted Mom to stay, she still packed up and went away, always looking her best when wearing her favorite dress. I'll never forget that summer green feeling, softer than anything could ever be. How could I not love her, seeing her so happy in her favorite color as I watched my mother, I left with my father and brother in time to catch the train, an item that remained as the train hissed and screeched to a sudden stop and vibrated the town with the loudest clunk. The whistle of the train would give goosebumps. The conductor opened the door and yelled, "All aboard!" Dressed in black with a white shirt and tie, he stepped down and gave the biggest sigh. Stepping so loud, boots that thumped, scaring the crowd. Again, on such an airy warm summer night it would make anyone shiver with fright. Once again, "All aboard" as he opened the doors, just as I wished, Mom kissed me on the lips. All I could remember was the smell of her lipstick that touched me forever. Without looking back. I felt lonely and ignored, the smell of the lipstick came back as it gave me quivers up my back, never waving goodbye, I cried and whispered, "I love you, Mom. Goodbye."

By Leon Breckenridge and Julie M. Wesner

Chapter 3

Honoring My Father

A few different neighbors watched me at times, including Mrs. Washington and Mrs. Carter. They were both my teachers. They would teach me about money and how to count and receive change from the store. When I went out to play, I loved being alone and would venture out into the woods and up into the mountains. It was very therapeutic for me, and I was hypnotized by the trees blowing in the wind. The sound of the water hitting the rocks from the stream nearby was music to my ears. I loved to dip my feet in the fresh, cold water. I would cup my hands together and reach down to scoop up the water to drink. The water was clear and so fresh it would take my thirst away on a hot summer day. I would look up at the high mountains, go up to the side and start climbing the rocks. I climbed so high that sometimes I didn't think I could get back down the steep mountain. It would be a long time before I figured out how to climb back down. I would walk around the woods for hours looking for fossils and find ones with the imprint of leaves in the slates.

One time while playing in the woods, I grabbed a long vine to swing across the woods like I saw in the *Tarzan* movies. The woods were like a big playground to me, and it became my favorite place to spend my time alone.

It would clear my mind from the past and bring back the fun and joy in me. Though there was one time when I did get startled. I heard something moving in the bushes and froze in fear of it being a bear or some kind of wild animal. All of a sudden two wild dogs walked out. Surprisingly they walked right up to me and brushed up against my legs. One was a short-haired dirty-white male and the other was brownish and was a female. I didn't hesitate to reach down to pet them, and they were friendly. They seemed to enjoy my company as I did theirs. There was something different about them, like they were sent to me for some reason. They were also very therapeutic to me and brought such joy into my life. I named them Whitey and Brownie. As the sun was going down, I knew it was time to head home. My dad always told me to be home before dark. I said goodbye to the dogs and hoped I would see them again. But as soon as I started to walk away, they followed me. They kept following me all the way to my house. They even climbed up onto my back porch with me and watched me go in.

The next morning, I went out and there they were lying on my porch. I gave my new pets some scraps. They seemed happy because they just stayed there. It was like they thought they were home and knew I'd be back. I walked downtown to the Montgomery supermarket and asked the butcher for some scraps. They must have been starving because when I fed it to them the scraps disappeared within seconds. After I started feeding them, they would follow me every time I left the house. I would take them for walks around town.

One day I decided to build a small log cabin in the woods. Most of the logs I found on the ground, but then I had to cut down some trees. I used logs from some birch trees, which gave the cabin an even nicer look. The neighbors sometimes threw out sheets of metal in their trash, and I used those for the roof. There was a time when I was walking the dogs around town and a boxer ran out toward us. The boxer and Whitey got into a fight. It was like he was protecting me. The boxer ran off and left us alone. When I got back home, my dad was there. I showed him my dogs and told him how I'd been feeding and playing with them. He didn't mind me having the dogs but was stern about me bringing them inside the house. His exact words were: "Dogs don't belong in the house." He also warned me about feeding them chicken bones because they could choke. I cleared out an area for them to sleep under our porch steps. I found some hay for them to sleep on and put boards around the area for shelter.

One night when Mrs. Price was watching my brother and me, I decided to let the dogs in to sleep with me in my bed. Mrs. Price didn't mind at all, and I doubt she told Dad about me bringing the dogs inside the house. Other times when Dad wasn't home, I would give my dogs a bath in our tub and they splashed and wagged their tails in enjoyment. I loved to make my dogs feel good. Their fur would shine and smell fresh like a spring breeze. Brownie and Whitey stayed with me for a couple of months, but one day I woke up and they were gone. I looked all around town and throughout the woods but never saw them again. At first it seemed strange to me that they were nowhere in sight, but then I knew for sure that they had been here for a reason. They were my best friends and they comforted me in a time of need. They were my angels.

Shortly after Mom left, Dad went away to Newark, New Jersey. I had a feeling he went to find Mom because he knew she had family there. Our upstairs neighbors, Mrs. Washington and Mrs. Price, would come over and watch us. When Dad got back, he seemed angry. I think he was hoping Mom would come back with him. His behavior changed, and he became very demeaning to Roy and me. He was constantly telling us what to do and what not to do, as if he was taking out his personal problems on us. When we didn't do what he said, he would call us names like knucklehead and hardhead. We weren't even allowed to go out and play anymore, but Roy and I would sneak out. One time we went out to play and heard Dad whistling for us. His whistle was so distinct, you couldn't miss it. I think the whole town heard it. We knew we were in so much trouble. As scared as we were, Roy and I ran home quickly. Dad's face was beet red as he stood there with fire in his eyes. He screamed at us with his whip in his hand. The whip was made out of a branch from a bush that we called a switch. It was the same thing the slave masters would use on blacks back in the day. He yelled, "Take off your clothes" and began to whip us. The beatings would last a good fifteen minutes but seemed like hours to me! We had welts across our backs, necks, and butts so bad that they would bleed at times. After the beatings he would send us to bed, and I'd find bloodstains on my sheets. The pain was so unbearable, it would last for weeks. Sometimes I just lay there wishing he was dead. When I woke, I would instantly remember falling asleep saying those words. I couldn't believe what I had said about wishing him dead and immediately I would pray to God. "Please don't take my father away," I would say. I continued to pray. "He is the only one I have to take care of me. My mom's gone. If something ever did happen to Dad, I would want a white family to adopt me." From reading magazines and watching TV, I saw how close and loving they seemed. They had everything you could ever need. But I learned that make-believe TV and reality can be two different things.

One time when Dad wasn't home, I saw my brother holding a gun to his head. I was scared and quickly ran over to him and tried to grab the gun from him. We struggled a bit and the gun spontaneously went off. Thankfully it was facing away from us at the time and the bullet put a hole in the floor. Somehow no one heard it because none of the neighbors came over. In shock we both stared at the floor. I then grabbed a candle and melted wax over the hole. If dad ever saw that hole, he would have beaten us worse than before.

The holidays were never the same after Mom left. Things change drastically. Thanksgiving wasn't much fun, but Dad would still make us dinner. He'd always hunt for squirrels and make a delicious squirrel dinner with mashed potatoes and gravy. Dad never gave us gifts again on Christmas. We never had a birthday party like other children. I always held onto the time that Dad gave me a baseball glove for no reason. I think it was because he loved baseball and I played it well. Dad loved making squirrel dinners, so we would still have a nice dinner to look forward to on Christmas. On Christmas Eve, Roy and I would go to church with Mrs. Price. I looked forward to it because a Santa Claus was there, and he would give out gifts after the service. I loved putting together the model airplanes made out of plastic. We spent most of the day there with other families such as Martins and our other neighbors. Afterwards, we would go back to our house with Mrs. Price and watch cowboy movies that she loved, such as *Gunsmoke*, *The Lone Ranger*, *Hopalong Cassidy*, and *The Roy Rogers Show*. When Christmas morning came, I was excited because the Christmas stories would be on television. Roy and I would watch the story of Jesus being born, which I loved as much as I loved the other Bible stories. Then we would watch the story about Santa Claus. Sometimes we would go out sledding down the big hill behind my house. We would go to other children's houses so we could play with their toys. Of course, I always wished I had all those toys and games, but nevertheless it was still fun. Some children had BB guns as toys. We would play with the cap guns. Afterward, we would play football. After a full day of playing, we would go back home to eat Dad's famous squirrel dinner.

Sometimes, Dad brought us to his friend Betty's house. Betty Kite was a tall, dark-skinned woman with tightly curled black hair. Dad never mentioned her previously, and even though I didn't know her that well, she was very nice to us. I was surprised I didn't know her, though, because she lived nearby. Dad might have been secretly dating her and just didn't want us to know. Betty was thoughtful to us, giving Roy and me presents. She bought us some kind of plaid flannel shirts. Of course, I appreciated the gift because she thought of us. Betty was a good cook, and she always made us a big dinner. She would either prepare turkey or ham, and her desserts were always the best. My favorite was her sweet potato pie. I must say Roy and I had a fun day even though we didn't get gifts like the other children. Other than Betty's gifts, the only other time Roy and I received gifts were from Aunt Gertrude, my mother's sister who lived in New Jersey. Mom stayed with her sister for a while after she left us. I believe Aunt Gertrude felt bad for us because Roy and I received a card from Mom with a dollar in it once in a while. Other than that, we didn't hear from Mom. I was still glad to know that Mom thought about us.

Outhouse, and the chicken in the backyard of Leon's grandmother's house

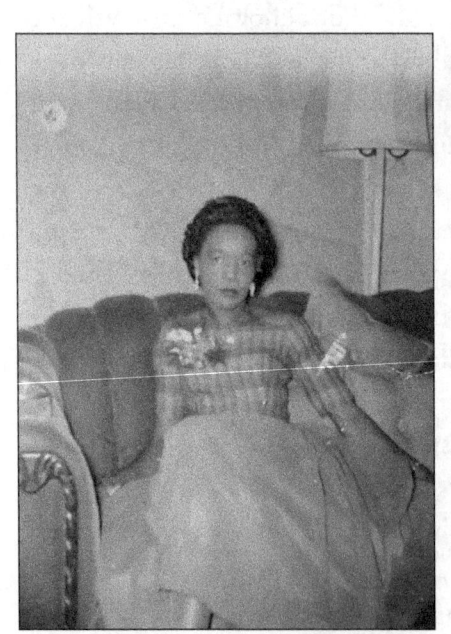

Betty Kite (the mother of Leon's older sister, Lori)

Aunt Gertrude (right), and her cook, Ethel (left)

CHAPTER 4

THE MOVEMENT THAT LEAD TO DESEGREGATION IN THE MONTGOMERY SCHOOL SYSTEM

IN 1954, A YOUNG BLACK GIRL NAMED LINDA CAROL BROWN started the Civil Rights Movement at the age of seven. The "Brown vs. Board of Education" lawsuit was filed in Topeka, Kansas. She wanted a better education and wanted to attend a white school. She went to a lawyer who eventually brought the case to be heard before the Supreme Court to prove the 14th Amendment was broken under the "Equal Protection Clause," which is a phrase in the 14th Amendment to the U.S. Constitution requiring that states guarantee equal protection of the law for all citizens. I was young and wasn't aware of this going on in the U.S. Supreme Court. I do recall looking across the way from my school (Simmons High School) and watching the white children play. I was amazed at the things they had. They had chain swings, a basketball court, and a basketball hoop out front. I always felt sad watching the children happily play. My school was all black from kindergarten to twelfth grade in one big building. All we had was a jump rope that we made from a clothesline and some chalk. We didn't have much to eat when we were at school. All we had was a brown bag lunch with a pickle, boiled egg, and bologna sandwich.

In 1957, we were finally allowed to go to the white school, which was like paradise to me. We attended the Montgomery grade school that taught students through the eighth grade. It was like attending a paradise school. They had freshly painted rooms with new blackboards, books, and desks. The gym was also clean and new. They had hot lunches with warm soup and even chocolate milk, which was my favorite. The school was much warmer than my old one because they had a new boiler. Simmons' boiler would shake the whole school at times and even set off the fire alarms. In the white school, all the white and black children were assigned kitchen detail at times, which meant cleaning the kitchen and washing the trays. The lunches cost twenty-five cents, but sometimes I would get them for free. Although it was supposed to be a better education, I didn't notice much of a difference in the way that the teachers taught. I loved the music class and really loved to sing. This school taught us how to dance. They only taught one dance called the "Three Step Dance." We had basketball games after lunch, and I was the captain most of the time and named my own teams. I liked Wolverine and Leopard as the names for our teams because they represented powerful animals, and it seemed easy for me to make friends. I enjoyed all the children and got along with them for the most part. The white girls were pretty because their hair was fine and their complexion was white, which especially caught my attention. We had so many opportunities at this school. If we got a "C" or better, we were allowed to be crossing guards. I loved wearing the white strap around me and even got to wear a badge. For school sports, I played basketball and my favorite, Little League. My dad gave me my first baseball glove. What a surprise because I never expected him to get anything from him. I was happy and excited to have my own glove.

About a month later, I tried out for the town's Little League. Over a hundred children tried out, but they only picked fifteen players, and I was selected as one of them. I couldn't believe it because I was the first black kid to make the team. I felt like Jackie Robinson, who was the first black man to make it to Major League Baseball. Our team was named after "Elks Furniture Store," and I played for a couple of years. I mainly played second base, but my coach, Charlie Bob Dotson, would put me in every position because I was a good player. Mr. Dotson would call me Little Henry because he knew my dad. He was nice to me, and I really liked him. He gave me rides to every practice and game in his late 1950s black and white Ford. Baseball was my favorite sport. I loved watching it and listening to it on the radio. Boy, did I love the Yankees because they were winners. Though I was already good at baseball, I got better and better as I played each day. Mr. Dotson told me I made the All-Star team. I was surprised to make the team at only age twelve.

Mr. Dotson told me I was batting over 600. We had a pitcher we called "Big Red" on our All-Star team because of his size. He could throw at least eighty miles an hour. One time during practice, he hit me in the back with a pitch. It knocked the wind out of me, and I went down to one knee. It was such a loud thump that Mr. Dotson came over and said, "Little Henry, it sounded like you didn't even have breakfast!" It took a few minutes, but I was able to get back up and keep playing. Our first All-Star game was against a team called "The Charleston," which is also the capitol of West Virginia. Red pitched a great game as usual, and I made a double play, but it was still a hard game for us. One of their players seemed to get them all right, because he hit a home run and won the game. We lost 1–0 and were completely out of the All-Star tournament.

Montgomery grade school was where I went to my first prom. I went with Shirley Jackson, a nice black girl who lived at the bottom of the hill from me. I knew the Jackson family well and liked them all. It was a nice dance. They served some punch and snacks. We did dances like the Mashed Potato, the Jerk, and the Twist. It was fun, and I loved to slow dance with Shirley. For some reason, eighth grade was the most difficult for me. I think I may have been distracted more and my thoughts wandered off a lot. I thought of my mom a lot and how much I missed her. I couldn't understand why we never heard from her. I still wandered off into the woods where I could think about everything that happened to us. One of those times, I saw a group of older girls sitting around a campfire, probably high school or college students. I hid behind the bushes and watched until suddenly some other girls snuck up behind me and grabbed me. They dragged me over to a tree and tied me up. Then they pulled my shorts down and played with my penis with large leaves that we called elephant leaves. The girls walked away and left me tied to the tree. All I could do was lay there and cry. Not too many people walk through these woods and I was worried that I'd be stranded there crying. Moments later, Mrs. Carter showed up and untied me. I was thankful she heard by cries. She walked me home, and neither she nor I said anything to anyone. Maybe she thought I would be embarrassed and not be ready to talk about it. I had a lot on my mind that year but did pretty well in school. My teachers didn't seem to agree because when I got my report card it read, "Repeat Eighth Grade." Boy, was I shocked and embarrassed. All I could do was cry on my way home and hide. For the first two weeks of the summer, I stayed indoors because I couldn't face anyone. When I returned to school the next year, I made sure I focused on my schoolwork.

I was thrilled to enter high school the following year. I remembered my freshman year, especially May 1960, when John F. Kennedy came to Montgomery. He was running for president. I was excited when I heard he was coming, and I couldn't wait to meet him. He spoke so distinguished, strong and powerful. He was dressed sharp and charismatic. Hearing him speak put me in such awe. I looked up to him. I was glad to see him elected that year.

My freshman year was exciting and different. I felt different, more grown up. We had more freedom than in elementary school. Though we got hot lunches, I liked to go downtown to the ten cents store and get a chili dog and Coke. The high school had a dress code, which made me feel more grown up. Getting dressed up was a fun time. I wore a nice collared shirt with dress pants, my dress hat-stingy brim (a dress hat), and my shiny black shoes. I liked high school and loved to impress the girls. They would put on sparkly, glamorous makeup and wear pretty skirts.

I was always good in sports. My freshman year I played basketball for the Greyhound Pups. I played football for the Montgomery High School team called "The Montgomery Greyhounds." We played every Friday night at a college football field that was next to my house. It was the Tech Football Field. We borrowed Tech's football field and they would borrow our gym until they built one. Everyone would dress up for our games.

Saturday afternoons we would all go watch the college football games. For some reason the children would fist fight after our games. It was always the blacks against the whites. Hundreds of people would come to watch the brawl, but no one would break it up. The teenage boys would fight until they couldn't get up or were badly hurt. I couldn't play sports my sophomore year because I developed knee problems. As I got older, my knee problems went away so I think it was growing pains. I was able to concentrate better in school, so I wouldn't stay back again.

In my junior year, I played football. I played so well that the coaches put me on varsity. The coaches had me play junior varsity one time. We played Oak Hill Red Devils, and I had over 300 yards and three touchdowns that game. That was definitely my best game. One of my assistant coaches, Mr. Williams, told me I was one of the best players he had seen in a long time. He couldn't understand why the head coach, Mr. C. E. Linham, didn't use me to start in any of the varsity games, and neither did I. The students called him Peter Head behind his back.

Our school had showers and, boy, was I happy because we hardly had water and gas at home. There wasn't even much for food at home either. My coach would satisfy my hunger, though, because he gave me money after each practice and game. I spent the money at my favorite places, McDonalds and Dairy Queen. This was the same year I started to work at the Montgomery supermarket. I would buy ten loaves of bread for a dollar and bring them home. Mr. Montgomery was very nice and generous. He gave me a pound of hamburger and bologna to take home for free.

Later in my junior year was when I started to date a girl name Phyllis. We dated the rest of that year and part of my senior year. Even though she lived eight to ten miles away, I would go to her house many times. I used to thumb or hitchhike for a ride up to Phyllis's house and I was able to get rides back home from someone at her home. Phyllis lived near a river, and we would always go down to the stream. Phyllis and I would play games with her whole family. We played card games and one was called "bid whist." Her family always had plenty of food. We ate meat, vegetables, and delicious desserts, like lemon meringue pie and pound cake with ice cream.

Phyllis's father worked hard as a coal miner. He made good money compared to us. They had a newer car and a beautiful house on the riverbank. It was a good size house with about five or six bedrooms because they had five kids. Mert, who was married to one of Phyllis's sisters, was very nice to me. He was on the police force in our town. Mert would invite me to come over to play some games. While I was still dating Phyllis, she got an emergency phone call at the office while we were in class. She had to leave because her father had a bad accident at the coal mine. Later I joined her at the hospital to see how her father was doing. He was cut up pretty bad around the lower stomach and groin area from a coal-cutting machine. It took him some time, but he did heal.

At times I would dread going home after school because all through high school up until my senior year, my dad still beat me. No one knew because I would just cover up the bruises and keep it to myself. Despite the physical abuse, my senior year was one of my favorites. I enjoyed school and always kept at least a "C" average to play sports and spent less time at home. Coach Dotson was my biology teacher. I enjoyed my English class because my teacher was polite. Her tests were hard, and one time I studied for a test for hours and got a ninety on it. I knew my English teacher was proud of me because she told the whole class. A West Virginia State administrator came to my school and talked to me and a girl named Ann Berry because our grades were good. The administrator wanted us to attend their state college. Some children from my school decided to go to the technology school, which was close to my house. At some point I wasn't interested in continuing school because I wanted to work and make some money. I couldn't wait to have the things I never had, like a nice car, house, and some real good food. I thought of how great it would be to have an easier life and a family of my own.

When I was not in school, I would sometimes visit my grandma and hear stories about my mom. During my senior year, I heard my mom was in town. I couldn't believe it because it had been four years since I last saw her. When I was downtown, someone told me they saw her at my grandmother's house. I ran six miles to my grandmother's house because I was so excited to see her. I missed my mom so much. It was impossible for me to forget about her. When I arrived at my grandmother's, I saw Grandma sitting in her swing on her front porch swinging as usual. I eagerly asked, "Where's mom?" She told me she was in the house. I quickly ran past her and into the house. Just like a little kid, I looked around yelling for her. I asked, "Where are you, Mom?" "Down here," she replied. Mom left when I was very young, and so in my mind she was much taller than me, but I was actually taller than Mom. Right away I ran into her arms, and we hugged each other. As we were hugging, I spotted a little girl about two years old come running around the corner and Mom said, "This is your little sister, Rose." Rose was short for Roseann. I was surprised that Mom moved on with her life and found someone else, and now I had a half-sister. I had always pictured my parents getting back together, but my hopes were dashed.

Grandma came in and said, "Leon, I heard your name on the radio. They called you 'Big Breck' and talked about your football games." The *Montgomery Herald* and the *Charleston Gazette* advertised me in their papers. Unlike my junior year, this time I was in the starting lineup. I made the "Honorable Mention Allstate" that year.

I stayed at Grandma's for dinner, but Mom didn't seem too interested in talking. I didn't know what to say or ask either. Mom seemed happy with Rose and her new life now. She appeared to enjoy being back in the area and at Grandma's house. I am sure she missed being there. When I got home, I never told Dad or Roy that I saw Mom. Dad might have gotten upset if I told him Mom was in town, and I didn't want to see Mom hurt him again. Roy was too busy with his friends and playing with the band anyway. Even though Dad didn't like it, Roy would get paid to play at proms and in clubs.

His band was good. They won talent shows and awards. The band's name was "Little Roy and the Orbits." During this time, Roy dated many females and fathered five children with a girl name Bonnie. Roy had to work many hours to support his growing family, so he never completed school like I did. I remember when Dad used to beat Roy because he wasn't happy with the way his life was going.

I heard Mom stayed at Grandma's for about five days, but I never went back to my grandmother to confirm this. I was busy with my life anyways. Besides being in school, I played football, had a girlfriend, and worked. It just wasn't the same seeing Mom again anyways. Our bond and love seemed to have changed, and we grew apart. It never changed that my grandma was my role model growing up. She was always good to me, and she often gave me money. Grandma looked out for me through good and bad times. I felt guilty about not visiting my grandmother much and about my distant relationship with my mother.

I continued dating, going to school, and playing sports. My senior year I played basketball. Coach C. E. Linham coached the basketball team. Even though our team didn't win any games, I knew I was good and did my best. I started in about six games, and then Coach Linham decided to replace me and put me on the bench. Randy Black was my replacement, and I noticed I was the only one replaced. Roy was also playing basketball with me, and he quit because I was replaced. After losing nineteen games, my friend Alfred Martin made the last shot in the last game and won it.

It was finally time for my senior prom, and I was looking forward to it. Phyllis was my prom date. The school set up the gym for the prom nicely. They served refreshments. The music was great, and we danced a lot. We did dances like the Jerk, the Mashed Potato, and the Watusi, which was the most popular. When Phyllis and I were having refreshments, someone came up to me and said Eddie Ferguson was there and wanted to see me. Eddie was an old friend who graduated a year before me. Phyllis had actually dated him in the past. The last time I heard from Eddie, he was on vacation in Detroit, so I was surprised he was there. Phyllis overheard our conversation about Eddie and got so excited that she ran ahead of me. I couldn't believe how Phyllis was acting. It was as if I wasn't even there. She grabbed Eddie by the arm and said, "Let's dance." I went right up to her, picked her up, and tossed her across the gym floor. She slid across the floor in her beautiful dress, and Eddie didn't stick around. It shook him right up. He went running out of there like a bat out of hell. Phyllis just screamed every curse word she could think of at me. Despite what had happened, I still wanted to be a gentleman and bring her home. We stopped at Dairy Queen on the way home like we planned, but neither of us said a word. I was heartbroken because I loved Phyllis. After that night, we didn't speak for weeks, although we saw each other in class.

One day I went downtown to have my favorite chili dog and Coke, and one of Phyllis's friends came running up to me and asked if Phyllis and I were engaged. She said Phyllis was showing off a ring on her finger bigger than my head. Of course, I was shocked because we certainly weren't engaged. I wondered who could possibly afford that ring. The next time I saw Phyllis was back in English class. She couldn't stop trying to get my attention by waving her hand in the air with the big dazzling ring. She thought she was smart, but I just ignored her and turned away. After class, I went up to Phyllis and asked if I could come over and talk about getting back together because I really missed her. She was just as happy as I was to do that. The next day I went over to her house and talked with her. She confessed to me that she had borrowed someone's ring to show off and make me jealous that she had a man in her life. We dated for a couple more years.

In 1967 I started working for a junkman. He had me chip away cement and bricks that were left from buildings being torn down. He would recycle the materials for us to use to build again. I made 25 cents per brick. One day my dad saw me and told me he didn't want me doing that type of work, especially for this man. I liked what I was doing, and this man paid me well, plus he was a nice man. I returned to work the next day and Dad saw me again. He said, "Didn't I tell you not to work for him?"

I had enough with my dad and stood up to him. I said, "You don't buy me clothes. I buy everything, even the bread and hamburger for us to eat." He just walked away without saying a word, which surprised me.

Later, my dad came back and put a gun to my head and said, "I'll blow your f***ing brains out if you ever talk to me like that again! Don't you talk to me that way." I threw everything down and went straight home. Boy, he really shook me. I was scared to death. It was like déjà vu reminding me of the time when Dad held a gun to my mom. Several days later, I decided it was time for me to get out of town and be an independent man.

Chapter 5

The Unexpected Journey

I decided to take a train to Newark, NJ, to see my mom and my aunts. What I really wanted was a fresh, new start somewhere else. I planned to get a good job and stay there. As soon as I arrived, I grabbed a cab and went straight to my aunt's house at 232 South 6th Street. I knew at this time my half-sister, Roseann, would be about twelve years old. Roseann was short, with short hair and a fair complexion. I reminisced about how much Mom loved music. I remembered her favorite song was "I Was Made to Love Her" by Stevie Wonder. My mom was like a vagabond, but by no means was it her fault. Mom came over with her new boyfriend, Percy, and Roseann. This was the first time I met Percy. I was shocked when I saw Mom, and I couldn't believe how bad Percy looked. Aunt Gertrude was embarrassed. It was extremely hot out, and they were dressed in long winter coats. I knew they both had serious mental illnesses, but I wasn't expecting this.

Aunt Gertrude didn't like Percy and the change in Mom, and neither did I. The way they looked and acted was embarrassing. Percy smelled like alcohol and slurred his speech. My mom also drank alcohol. We couldn't even have a normal conversation. What a visit. Since I planned on staying at Aunt Gertrude's for a while, I got a summer job. It was a job teaching children how to play sports, so of course I enjoyed it because I loved sports.

One day Aunt Gertrude asked me to go and check on my mom, Roseann, and Percy. She was concerned and did her best to look after everyone. When I got to my mom's apartment, it was as horrible as them, or maybe even worse. It was infested with cockroaches. Their clothes and trash were piled up to the ceiling, and their kitchen was covered in grease. Two malnourished kittens came running out. They were probably looking for food because they were excited to see me. At this visit I didn't see Roseann. She must have left to live with someone, like our cousins. I left and decided to go back the next day to see if I could clean their apartment a little. I did the best I could but decided to just let them be because they both needed serious psychiatric or psychological help.

Between July 12 and 17, 1967, a riot broke out. I heard it was because the police beat a black man. There was chaos for four days straight. There was looting and property damage all over the city. They burned down an A&P store down the street from Aunt Gertrude's house. One day while walking, I saw three or four black men grab bats and hit a white guy on the head several times. I got out of their way because I was scared to death. Another day I decided to call Phyllis and went to the nearest phone booth. While making the call, a store alarm went off next to me. All of a sudden four or five state police officers pulled up and pulled out their guns. They aimed them right at me and said, "What are you doing here? Get off the streets, boy!" I slammed that receiver down so fast and ran as fast as I could to Aunt Gertrude's house to ask for money to leave town. Everything was out of control, and I wasn't going to live in the middle of this craziness anymore. Although things started to calm down and the riot finally came to an end, I still wanted to get on the next Greyhound bus and go home. It was a horrible thing to see hundreds of people get injured. Twenty-six people died due to the riot.

It was nice being back in my hometown. At least it was quiet, but most of all I had Phyllis. Phyllis was the first person I went to see. I really missed her and her family. Of course, I told Grandma I was back home, and boy, was she happy to see me. I don't know who was happier to see me, Phyllis or my grandma. I saw Roy, and he was pretty busy with his new life. He worked a lot because he had a wife and five children. I felt bad he never finished school because he was too busy having children, and having a good-paying job would require some high school education.

One time at home I decided to watch a marine movie called *To the Halls of Montezuma* and for some reason I really took to the movie. What an impulse and desire I got to be a marine then. After the movie, I went running across the hill and saw my neighbor, Hazel. "I want to be a marine," I said to her.

Hazel had a shocked look on her face and said, "What's wrong with you, boy? You a black man. After basic training, they'll send you to Vietnam and you'd get killed, boy."

I went to take the Air Force exam. On October 2, 1967, I went to basic training at Lockland Air Force base in Texas. The first two weeks I did well. It wasn't long before I became squad leader. One of the drill instructors liked me and allowed me to be a leader. This one French-Canadian instructor didn't like me for some reason and put me at the back of the squad. A couple of days later, he called me into his office and told me he almost sent me back to basic training. For some reason I was the only one he picked on, and for no reason he always tried to find something wrong with me. I did well in training though and always obeyed my instructors, so I knew he never would like me, maybe because I was black. There was no way I was going back to basic training. I was determined to keep doing well and move forward. I was excited on graduation day and thought everyone in our flights did well. Unfortunately, one guy was out of step, so we didn't win an award. After graduation I was sent to the Chanute, Illinois, Air Force base for a couple of years. I was part of the security police and worked the gates. One day while working the front gates, two girls pulled up in a convertible wearing short skirts, and they started flirting with me. I then saw a detail sticker on their car and let them through. That night while I was still working the gate, everyone was driving around really fast and cars were flying by me. Everyone was in a panic. So, I called my sergeant, Joe, and he told me that Martin Luther King had been shot in Tennessee earlier that day. I never forgot that night, April 4, 1968. It was an upsetting and somber night. I liked Martin Luther King and looked up to him.

One afternoon I was in a terrible car accident. The guy I was riding with ran a stop sign, and I was hurt badly. I was taken by ambulance to the hospital emergency room. The medical staff took x-rays and told me I fractured my pelvis. The hospital called my base, and Dr. Bruce Dixon, a captain, came down a couple hours later. I had met him one time while working the gate, and we became friends. Dr. Dixon looked after me and became my doctor while in the hospital. They gave me morphine for the pain, which I must admit I liked. They also gave me some dopamine. A couple of weeks later, I was discharged and had to use crutches for a few weeks. About a week after I was discharged, Dr. Dixon invited me to his house for dinner. I was impressed, because he made us a delicious steak dinner with potatoes and fine wine. Although I was full, I could not resist the dessert, a fresh baked apple pie with ice cream topping. After dinner, Dr. Dixon showed me his photo album. It seemed odd to me because it was just random pictures of men. He took a picture of me and became extra friendly toward me. I never knew he was gay until I was out of the Air Force. Even then, he kept writing to me and asking me to visit him.

As time passed by, I started feeling better and I was still getting paid by the military while I was out for about a month. A few months later, I got orders that I would be going to Vietnam. I wasn't worried about it, but I wanted to go home first and see everyone since I did not know what my future held once I got deployed. I requested permission to go home for two weeks, and it was allowed. By then Phyllis had moved to Washington, DC, for an operators job. I visited my grandma and gave her my address. I was able to visit the rest of my family and many friends before I had to return to the base. Before I was deployed to Vietnam, I was sent to the Lackland Air Force base in Texas. I took the AZR course for combat duty and was trained in using guns and grenades for two weeks. Then off I went to Cam Ranh Bay in Vietnam. It was so hot, and the temperature reached approximately 120 degrees Fahrenheit. My skin got much darker, like a solid black charcoal.

The base where I was stationed was off the South China Sea. I was part of the security police, so I stayed mainly on the base. The other military soldiers and I would go swimming a lot to keep cool. It didn't take long to get hot again with those scalding temperatures. Even though we were on the base, we still were dealing with rockets being shot at us by North Vietnam. Every time we were being attacked, we had to jump into our foxhole for protection. The foxhole was a small pit below the surface of the ground used for cover from the enemies or when we were under attack.

I lived with a group of white guys in my barracks. The African American guys didn't like that because we were treated differently because of our race. The black guys would call me an Oreo or Uncle Tom, and the black guys would call the white guys rabbits. The black guys would beat them up and say they were no good white devils. I would always defend the white guys even though they treated me like I was inferior to their race. Finally, I moved in with the other African Americans guys because they wouldn't stop harassing me for living with the white guys.

While I was serving in the military, Phyllis and I decided to break up because we couldn't see each other anymore. There was so much that changed in both of our lives, but we still remained friends. The guys would tell me stories about how I could go into the village and get a girl for five or ten dollars. They showed me a hole under the fence and told me I could crawl under it to get to where the girls were hanging out. They told me they would look out for me and help me sneak back in when I got back. Well, I was shocked when I got back because they were pointing guns at me. They said I was off limits and called the Air Force police. I just cursed at them and ran back to my barracks. Air Force police came to my door and said that the first sergeant wanted to see me. They cuffed me and took me to him. I was released from the police and into his custody. I was given an Article 15, which is a demotion for violating the Air Force rules.

Two weeks later, I had to see my commander, who was a four-bird colonel. He stripped me of all my stripes, back down to nothing, and fined me $300. He asked me if I wanted to explain myself, and of course I took the opportunity. I told him the whole story of how the guys set me up. He actually took it into consideration and dismissed me by taking away one stripe and forgiving the fine. This taught me that not everyone means well and not everyone is your friend. However, this punishment did not clear me because I was still put in protective custody for two weeks. I was placed into a cell that was in his office and the door was left open so I could still go back and forth to my duties. My duties required a lot of standing and overtime, and my legs started bothering me again. The doctors said I couldn't do that kind of work anymore due to the pain from standing, so I took a test for administrative work and passed. I worked at the post office for a couple of months before I got my orders to go back to America. They were sending me to Pease Air Force Base in Portsmouth, New Hampshire. Before I went to New Hampshire, I requested leave to go back home. It was late at night when I arrived home, but I made sure I visited everyone throughout my stay. First, I saw my dad, Roy, and Bonnie, Roy's wife, and she did not hesitate to send me care packages with warm, inspirational letters in them. I had to go see my loving grandma, of course, because I loved to visit with her. She had always thought of me and sent me care packages. She sent me her special cookies with meaningful notes inside. I always sent her money to help her for all she had done for me growing up. My grandma was excited to show me what she did with the money. I thought she'd use it for bills and food, but she saved it. Grandma never had a bathroom or running water in her house, and sure enough she had a new bathroom put in with the money I sent to her. It was well spent on herself and for others, and for that I was so happy. Unlike Grandma, my dad didn't save the money I sent. He was supposed to save it for me so I could have money to spend when I got home. I had asked him to put aside the money so I could save for a car. When I arrived at his house, my dad opened the door and immediately said, "I'm going to pay you back." I told him not to worry about it because he obviously needed it more than I needed a car.

It felt good being back in my hometown and seeing everyone, but even my two-week leave went by quickly. Soon after I was back on base, I decided not to bother sending my dad any more money. I figured I would save my own money from now on. This was my sense of independence and responsibility. While on base I decided to pick up a side job to save more money. I really wanted my own car. It made me feel free not having to rely on anyone for a ride. For a while I worked as a waiter at the NCO Club (Non-Commissioner Office). It was fun being a waiter because a lot of girls went there, and I was intrigued by their company. I dated a lot of the girls that frequented the club.

After I saved enough money to buy my first car, I saw a nice 1965 Pontiac Bonneville for sale. They wanted $900 for it, and I had exactly enough tucked away for it. It made it a lot easier to date when I had a car because somehow girls seemed to think a man with a car meant he had money. Once I purchased the car, I decided to look for a better job. I took interest in the procurement office. People there would bid for spaces on the base to use for their business. I was a typist, so the stigma that woman mainly hold typist jobs was defunct. I was not exclusively working as a typist. I also worked on the computer system, plus I picked up and delivered mail.

Sgt. Norman came up to me one day and asked me to march in the Alan Shepard Jr. Parade. Alan Shepard Jr. was an American astronaut, naval aviator, test pilot, and a businessman. He was the first American to travel in space. He walked on the moon in 1971 and hit a golf ball off the surface of the moon. He was born November 18, 1923, in East Derry, New Hampshire, where the parade was held. It was a nice day for the parade because the temperature was not cold, and the weather was clear. I was proud to participate in the parade. Derry, New Hampshire, was a beautiful place, and the beaches were so warm and clean. Salisbury beach was the closest to our base. It was one of my favorite places to go to be alone and think. I went there a lot to meditate and to enjoy the scene. One day, as I was enjoying the great weather, a woman and I sparked up a conversation. Her name was Linda and she seemed like a nice woman. We started walking along the shore, talking and getting to know each other. Time flew by as I enjoyed the conversation with her. I took her to get a drink and something to eat at a nearby club. It was pleasant being around her, and we danced most of the night away. I learned Linda was from Salem, Massachusetts, which wasn't too far from my base. She came to Derry quite often because she also loved Salisbury beach. Before it was time for us to leave, we exchanged phone numbers. Around the time I met Linda, I got an honorable discharge on October 2, 1971, after my four years of service.

Leon in Derry, New Hampshire, at the Air Force base

Chapter 6

The Witch City

Linda and I moved in together and lived together for about two years. The relationship was going well for me, but Linda really wanted to get married. I didn't want to settle down yet because I did not feel I was ready to get married. Marriage was a big step, and I knew I wanted to do more with my life before I settled down.

Linda decided to get in touch with an old boyfriend who had moved to New York. I was surprised because I thought things were fine just the way we were living. I guess she really wanted to settle down with someone because she went to stay with him. I had to accept her choices. I missed her but marriage wasn't for me at least at that point. I kept the apartment for a few years after she left. I kept busy working and meeting a lot of friends. I liked working as a security police officer, but after a few years the program ended, and I had to look for another job. It wasn't hard for me to find other jobs because I had a lot of experience. I found a security job at Salem Hospital, and I got along with everyone I encountered. The job was good because it offered great healthcare benefits. The nurses were friendly, but one in particular named Susie took a liking to me. She invited me to her surprise birthday party that the other nurses hosted for her. What a party!

There was a performance by the Chippendale dancers. Susie, the birthday girl, came up to me and said, "I thought you were going to be one of the dancers." It surprised me because I never showed any interest in dancing provocatively. She told me I should be a model. She got me thinking about modeling. I had heard about the Red Book for actors and models and decided to look into it because I was curious.

One day I got a call from the sheriff, Bob E. Cahill. He asked me if I would like to come work for the sheriff's department and be a deputy sheriff. I was excited but curious about how he had heard about me. He told me it was through the police department. He heard I did such a good job when I went through that program, so he wanted me to work for the sheriff's department. I did not hesitate saying yes right away, without even thinking about my job at Salem Hospital. He said I could get sworn in right away because of my experience with the service and police programs. I knew I had to put in my notice at Salem Hospital immediately. I enjoyed my time working there with everyone and made sure I said goodbye to them all. I was there for a couple of years and met great friends.

I knew working for the sheriff's department would be a good career opportunity. I was told I would be working the 3 p.m. to 11 p.m. shift at the Lawrence jail. Boy, was that one of the worst jails I've ever seen. It was so old and broken down that they didn't even have any running water in the bathrooms. The inmates had to use what they called white wax buckets to go to the bathroom. When the inmates got mad, they would throw feces and urine at the guards. Despite having buckets of waste hurled at you, I still liked being a deputy sheriff and working with the other guards for a couple of years before I considered putting in for a transfer. I tried to ignore the asinine behavior of the inmates. I didn't let their complaining and causing trouble jeopardize my work. I didn't blame them for complaining about the condition of the jail and their living situation because it was substandard and inhumane. I thought the sheriff's department would fix up the jail a little since it was such an old, broken-down building with barely standing walls. It was built around the time of the Battle of Waterloo in June 1815.

After a couple of years working in Lawrence, I put my transfer in for the Salem jail since I lived in Salem, Massachusetts. The jail wasn't any better than Lawrence's jail, but at least it was within walking distance of my house so I did not require transportation. I stayed at the Salem jail for about twelve years. Though I appreciated the convenient location, over the years I decided to look for a better apartment because I was making more money due to increased wages. I treated myself and bought an old but nice front-wheel-drive Oldsmobile Toronado I found a really nice townhouse in a peaceful area in Peabody, which was a short drive to work. I moved into the condo and made Peabody my new residence. One day while I was at work, Sheriff Cahill asked me if I wanted to get a boxing team together with some of the inmates in Salem. He knew I had boxed in the Air Force, but I was surprised he asked me. He was going to get a team together in Lawrence, so we could have a boxing match there because they had a boxing ring there. I got some guys together who were interested and began training them at the jails. I got permission to take them on runs along the ocean in Lynn. The inmates were good and never attempted to run off. They stayed with me because they were happy getting to go out and enjoyed the fresh air. They benefited from the training because they were able to work and feel better about themselves, and they were excited to participate in the match.

The inmates and I started going to the Harbor House in Lynn to practice boxing. The Harbor House was a bar and club that we got permission to use at times. After a couple of months of training, we held the match. Well, the match didn't go as planned because a riot broke out between the inmates. I didn't know at the time but one of my guys had stolen whiskey from the club and got caught with it at the Salem jail. Between both of those incidents, the program was canceled. Shortly after the riot, Sheriff Cahill had to resign because he had a major heart attack. It was probably best for him to resign because it was a stressful job. We remained friends throughout and kept in touch. Deputy Reardon was second in charge, therefore, he ran for sheriff and won. I missed the presence of Sheriff Cahill because he treated me respectfully and was good to me. He acknowledged my outstanding work. Sheriff Reardon, on the other hand, didn't pay much attention to me. I approached Sheriff Reardon in the hopes he would grant me a promotion after I told him about my experience and my degree. He didn't seem to be interested in what I had to say.

One day while I was doing my rounds, I had an incident with a black inmate. I didn't know him too well because he was fairly new. He was being held in custody until his court date because he was charged with armed robbery and murder at the St. James Credit Union. While doing my rounds, this guy and some of the other inmates were out of their cells for a while. For some reason this one inmate was following me, so I stopped doing my rounds and went up to him to asked, "What are you up to?"

He responded, "I want to go around to the other side of the jail."

I told him, "You are not allowed to." Then he kicked me hard in my head, which caught me off guard, and my keys went flying in the air, along with me landing flat on the concrete. I was pretty out of it and disoriented and was taken by ambulance to Salem Hospital. I was in and out of it most of the time. Dr. Paeli was the neurologist that ran tests immediately. I was admitted because I was still a little disoriented and suffered a serious concussion. All I could remember about the incident was the ambulance ride and being kept in the hospital for about a week. While I was recuperating, I heard from another guard that I was blamed for the whole incident. A white guard went to the sheriff and defended the inmate. I was not asked my side of the story when I went back to work. The sheriff switched me to the night shift. I sure wasn't happy because I felt I was being punished for no reason for something that was instigated by the inmate.

A couple of weeks after I was kicked in the head and my shift was changed, I went to the National Association for the Advancement of Colored People (NAACP). I talked to Clarence Jones, who was the president. He advised me to write a report and explain the whole incident in as much detail as possible. I felt relieved because I would finally be able to explain my side of the incident. When my ink touched the paper, I felt even better. After the president read my report, he immediately got on the phone and dialed the sheriff. Jones defended me without hesitation and strongly told the sheriff I didn't do anything wrong. Jones ordered the sheriff to put me back on days immediately or there would be hell to pay. I appreciated the president stepping in, and I thanked him. Upon my return to work, I was assigned back to my regular day shift. While I worked at the Salem jail, I decided it was in my best interest to go back to school. I went to North Shore Community College (NSCC) in Lynn and graduated with a sociology degree around 1976. During the time I attended NSCC, a friend from the college introduced me to a woman named Charlotte. She was a teacher at Lynn Tech and taught Distributed ED, which was a class for students to learn typing, business, and math. Charlotte was a stunning and beautiful medium-built woman. She had a fair complexion and her smile sparkled like spring water. Her nose was straighter than an arrow. Charlotte's wore her hair in loose curls and it was soft as cotton. I began dating Charlotte shortly after meeting her.

I dedicated twelve years to working for the sheriff's department, and I decided I wanted to do something different. As part of my change, I took the U.S. Postal Service exam. I eagerly waited for an answer from the postal service because I was getting burned out from the sheriff job. While I worked at the Salem jail waiting to find another job, I continued to date Charlotte. I proposed to her because I was not getting any younger. We decided to get married. We got married on April 12, 1980, at the St. Stephens Episcopal Church in Lynn. It was a big wedding with attendees from both of our families and the guards I invited from the jail. Our reception was at the Holiday Inn in Peabody and our honeymoon was in Spain. Charlotte's uncle owned a condo in Spain near the beach, and he allowed us stay there. Spain was a beautiful place and different from the atmosphere where I lived. However, Spain was a little cold at that time. France wasn't too far from where we stayed, so we drove there to visit for a day.

While it was quite an experience working in Salem and living in Peabody, I often reminisced about my younger years in West Virginia. I thought about my brother, Roy, my grandmother, and my aunts. Most importantly, I thought about my father. I often wondered how he was doing. I knew he had a girlfriend and that was just about the only information I knew about him. I felt distant from my father after moving out of state. I wish I had checked on him more frequently than I had. In May 1981, I got a call from his girlfriend. It was not a call I was expecting. She told me that it was Mother's Day and she had not heard from my father, and he failed to show up for work. She called the police for them to do a wellness check on him. The police found my father's body. My father committed suicide by taking a bullet to his head. I never knew my father was severely depressed. I wished I had seen the signs of mental illness, but he hid them. Maybe the loneliness drove him to death. I dreaded going to my father's funeral because that would be my final memory of him, in a casket. The worst part about my father's death is that he took his life, and it was not an accident or a natural death.

Chapter 7

Post Office

I FINALLY HEARD FROM THE POSTAL SERVICE ABOUT A MONTH after taking the exam, and I got hired. I started as a mail handler in Chelsea and did that for about ninety days. I then became a carrier, and I delivered in Everett, Chelsea, East Boston, Winthrop, and Revere. I really didn't like it as much, so I asked my supervisor if I could go back to a mail handler, which I did. For some reason another employee, a white male, became jealous of me and harassed me for about four months. I found out he was mad because I got the day shift before him. Even though we had different shifts, we still worked a couple hours in the same area. Many times, he stared me down with the look of envy.

One day he was driving a Gitney, which is a machine used to pull mail. All of a sudden, he pulled up next to me and spit right at me. He barely missed me as it landed right in front of my foot. Then he called me a nigger. I went right after him, and he ran right into the manager's office screaming, "Get this nigger away from me!" I told the manager what he did, and the inspectors came to me a few days later. Once I told them what happened, he was transferred right away.

I worked as a mail handler for approximately three years and then put a bid in to work at the airport post office. I was promoted to a mail handler technician, which meant I had a little more authority and got a raise. I was also a supervisor because there were some guys who worked under me. One day when I was sorting mail, I heard that Susan, one of our employees, got murdered. I was shocked. She was stabbed in the throat thirty times and thrown into the trunk of a car. I heard she was involved in some kind of credit card fraud or scam. They never found out who murdered her. It seemed like a white-collar crime. I wondered if it had something to do with the guy I saw her with because she was killed two days after I saw them together. I just could not stop thinking about it. Susan was a kindhearted and beautiful Italian woman. I remembered going to a bar one night to pick up money that someone collected from our softball team. She saw me and asked me to join her friends, but I left because I did not like all the smoke in there. I never mentioned it to anyone, but now I wish I did because you never know if it could have made a difference in solving her murder. I sorely missed Susan's presence at the post office because she made working there lively.

Even though I'd been able to walk all these years, I'd noticed my hip hurting off and on from that car accident I was in during my time in the service. I'd still see Dr. Sweetland from time to time at Salem Hospital. Every time I saw him, he would ask me about my hip and take x-rays yearly. He knew I would have to have a hip replacement eventually. After a few years of working at the airport, I asked to be transferred to the General Mail Facility post office for a better position with more pay. It was a level 5 job, and I was in control of driving a Gitney.

I was working in Boston and knew there were casting companies in the area because of all the films being made in Boston then. I decided to look into it because of what the nurse at Salem Hospital had told me about modeling. I inquired into the casting companies. I got my headshots together and began mailing them out to companies. I got a call from one of them and was assigned as an extra for *Spencer for Hire* for most of their filming in town. I enjoyed working with the casting company, so I continued working with them. I was an extra for quite a few casting companies for a few years. I was in a few other films, such as *Guest of Low*, *Field of Dreams*, and *Maverick Square*. I did a lot of work for Angela Peri, the owner of Boston Casting. One big film I was in was *Forgotten Genius*, a true story about the scientist Percy Julian. For the most part, I just did extra work and had a line here and there. My biggest paying job was an Industrial Business commercial. I didn't have any lines but dressed as a businessman based on their criteria. They paid me a couple thousand dollars for it.

It wasn't long after I started at G.M.F. that Charlotte got pregnant with my first son, Henry, who was named after my father. On August 6, 1982, Henry was born at Salem Hospital. I was excited and handed out cigars to my friends that day. Seeing my first child being born was like a miracle to me. He was a big baby with very little hair, but to me he was like a little man. It was so different but exciting having a baby around. I loved to hold him and would stare at him and admire him. It was such a loving feeling to have my own son. Henry was baptized at the First Baptist Church in Salem. We had some family and friends over to the house for a small gathering. When Henry got a little older, someone did a dedication for him at the St. Stephens Episcopal Church in Lynn. Therefore, Henry was baptized there as well, making it his second baptism.

Growing up, Henry became interested in sports. He tried soccer first. He seemed to like playing with the other kids, and he did well at it. Henry always wanted to do his best at everything he tried. I wanted Henry to have good balance and focus on everything he did, so I put him into ballet classes. I even bought him black tights for his first class. Henry didn't like the idea of taking ballet classes. He didn't want to leave the house to go on the first day. I had to carry him out of the house. His exact words were, "I don't want be a movie star." Well, he changed his mind quickly when he saw a class full of girls.

Henry lost interest in soccer because he wanted to play football. He started playing Pop Warner football. He loved football and was disappointed when the season was over. Henry would've kept playing if he could. Spring Little League came up, and Henry played for the Peabody Pirates.

He decided he was going to play football and baseball only, and that's what he did growing up. Football was always his favorite, and he played it well. Henry enjoyed playing baseball during the off season, though, and did extremely well. I wish I could have coached some of Henry's teams, but I worked a lot of nights when he was younger. I made an attempt to attend many of his games.

Henry played baseball and football throughout his teenage years. He went to Bishop Fenwick High School. While playing football one year, his team made it to the state championships and won. I was so proud of him and his teammates because they worked hard to get there. In the spring while playing baseball, his team won the All-Stars Award. There were colleges interested in Henry at that point, but his grades kept him from being accepted. After high school Henry went to Cushing Academy in Ashburnham, MA, for a year to get his grades up. His baseball team did so well they got a road trip to Arizona for a week to play against several Arizona teams. The trip to Arizona was just for fun, not for a tournament or championship. They were in the division game with Lawrence Academy and played at Holy Cross in Worcester. It was a tough game. Both teams played well, although they lost the game. After completing Cushing Academy, Henry went to East Stroudsburg University for four years. He graduated with a business management degree. All four years Henry played football and was placed in division two. During college, Henry was five feet, ten inches, and weighed 240 pounds. He was the inside linebacker. A lot of their games were played in Pennsylvania, where they won a couple of championships.

Almost two years later on July 9, 1984, after my first son was born, my second son, Robert (Robbie) was born at Salem Hospital. He was a big baby and a quiet one. I loved him just as much as my first. I was still working a lot of late shifts and couldn't spend as much time with my children as I wanted. Robbie and Henry got along well but didn't play much together. They seemed to like doing their own thing. I wanted to get them involved into some extracurricular activities. I signed them both up for karate, which was Korean style. I was only able to let them do it for a couple of months because of my work schedule. Robbie tried Pop Warner at age ten but didn't like it. In middle school he played basketball, and after school he played triple A Little League and Babe Ruth. My schedule changed, and I was able to coach both of his baseball teams. Robbie looked forward to the fall because basketball was his favorite. He did well in basketball, but his team didn't win any awards those years. His AAA Little League team won the city championship and then went into Little League and won the League Championship. I taught Robbie to play several positions. He loved to play shortstop, but he would also pitch and play catcher.

After middle school, Robbie played for the AAU Team in Salem, which stands for American Amateur United team. I paid about $300 for him to play, but for some reason his coach didn't let him play much as well as some other teammates. I started my own AAU team because of the way the coach treated my son. Robbie played for a year and his teammates played extremely well each year. We played Springfield in Newark, New Jersey, for the championship, which we won. Robbie went to Fenwick Catholic School in Peabody, MA, for freshman year. He really didn't like it, so for his sophomore year he went to Peabody High School. He continued playing basketball and became captain. Even though his team played well, they didn't win anything until their senior year. That year they played North Attleboro at Salem High for the state championship and won.

After high school, Robbie went to North Shore Community College to study business for a year. He wanted to get his grades up before going to the University of Massachusetts Lowell, which he did the following year. He played basketball while attending all four years and made it to one tournament but lost. After the four years, Robbie graduated with a business degree. I'll never forget this one night when we were all sitting around the dinner table. Robbie said to me, "You know, I wouldn't be here if it weren't for you." I was so happy to hear that and to know my son not only recognized what I did for him, but he really appreciated it.

A couple years after Robbie was born, my third son, Daniel, was born on November 2, 1986. Daniel wasn't born at Salem Hospital like my other sons due to complications. Charlotte hemorrhaged and had to be rushed to St. Margaret's Hospital in Boston. I was thankful to the doctors and nurses for everything they did to make sure Charlotte and my son were safe. Daniel was born premature, and Charlotte stayed in the hospital for about two weeks. Both of them did just fine. Daniel grew up as a normal child. He knew how to crawl, walk, and talk at the appropriate times a baby would. Growing up, he was athletic like his brothers. Daniel started off in T-ball around four or five years old. He played baseball around eight or nine years old for Little League. I coached his team for the four years that he played. Daniel liked being the catcher. Our team did well and played for some championships. When Daniel became a sophomore, he played Babe Ruth for Peabody. I coached the Little League Championship, and everyone received trophies. Daniel was picked to play for the All-Star team a couple of times, and he received a lot of trophies. He loved baseball, and he played for St. Mary's at the same time. Daniel attended St. Mary's for all of his high school years. In the fall he played football for St. Mary's but injured his knee. He was out for the rest of the season. Eventually he needed surgery, so he couldn't play any sports during his junior year. Daniel was eager to play again in his senior year, and he looked forward to it. The baseball team didn't win anything that year, but his football team did. Daniel became the captain, and his football team won the state championship that year.

After high school, Daniel went to North Shore Community College for a year and studied business. He wanted to go there to improve his grades. I knew someone at Mt. Ida College in Newton, MA, and got him a scholarship for four years, which was called the President's Award. Daniel decided not to continue with his education, though. He wanted to work at the Peabody Essex Museum, which he did for a little over a year. He worked as a security officer before he became a supervisor. Unfortunately, Daniel started to go down a dark path that was unseen to me. He became friends with people that were using and abusing drugs, and he indulged in it himself, which led to years of trouble for him and heartache for the family. He would steal things from us and sell and pawn them to have money to buy drugs to support his bad habit. Daniel has been struggling with this since his early twenties. He got addicted to OxyContin. He was having a lot of knee pain from that old injury back in high school and just started to take it. Prescription drugs can be beneficial for pain but truly destructive in the long run once someone gets addicted to them. It is hard to break the habit, and it can be a long and painful road to recovery, if it is possible to recover. Charlotte and I love Daniel and are always here for him. We pray for him to fully recover.

Our family was financially stable and pretty much well off. Charlotte and I were considering having another child after Daniel because I really wanted a girl. We decided it was best to adopt a child. One day in 1994, we were watching our local CBS channel when they aired *Wednesday's Child*, and we saw a beautiful six year old girl named Ashley. She was singing "Amazing Grace." Ashley was so sweet and beautiful and had such a lovely voice. Charlotte and I loved her and wanted to adopt her, so we called the number that was displayed on the television screen right away. The process took between six and eight months with a lot of paperwork and even some court dates, but it was well worth it. We got to meet Ashley and take her out a few times. We took her out to eat and then bowling afterward. Ashley appeared to enjoy bowling. We had a great time spending time with her.

During the adoption process, I wasn't feeling like my usual self. I was feeling tired and weak every day. I scheduled a doctor's visit and went to see my primary care doctor. After a few tests, he told me my blood count was low and he made an appointment for me to see an oncologist. I saw Dr. Robert Wagner in Lynn, and he gave me a bone marrow test. It took about a week to get the results because he sent it to Boston, which was outside of the North Shore area. Charlotte was concerned and went with me for the follow-up visit. We were both shocked when we got the news. The doctor said I tested positive for hairy cell Leukemia. The feeling that went through me is indescribable. I felt even weaker and devastated. Neither one of us knew what to say because we were lost for words. It was extremely upsetting and sad for us as we slowly walked out of the office in silence with no sense of direction. We went home, and I went straight to my Bible. I read Matthew 5:19 out loud in my head until I fell asleep. When I woke up, I swear I saw Jesus standing over me and he touched me. I knew then by my vision of Jesus that it was a sign I was going to be healthy again and I should not worry.

I decided to get a second opinion at the Veterans Hospital (VA). Unfortunately, I got the same test results. We checked the Agent Orange list for that type of Leukemia so I would be able to be compensated, but it wasn't on the list. I never gave up, though, as I went through a series of treatments. The VA worked hard and went through a number of channels to get my treatments for Leukemia approved. It finally got approved about twenty years later through the Obama administration. I was so thankful for the VA doing all the hard work to get this approved. I went back to Dr. Wagner to see about treatment. He said my blood count and platelets were too high, so he had to treat that first. Once my levels were back down, they put me in the hospital to start chemotherapy. I was so thankful that I never got sick during my whole treatment since I had heard of people getting sicker and losing their hair. About a week later, I was allowed to go home with a chemo pump. It was easy to use because the pump was automatic and easy to operate. It was just a small machine that was attached to me, and I was able to walk around and go outside. About two weeks after using the pump, a nurse came and picked it up. My hip was feeling much better after the treatment. My doctors wanted to make sure my blood levels were fine so they could replace my hip. My blood count was lower, and I had hip surgery. I was only in the hospital for a day and went home on crutches. A few weeks later, I was able to use a cane.

Because of my medical issues prior to VA getting approved, the social workers for Ashley's adoption were concerned and asked us if we still wanted to adopt. Charlotte and I didn't hesitate when we said yes. We had already spent time quality time with Ashley and loved her like our own, plus we didn't want to disappoint her. Ashley was always happy to see us, so we knew she was looking forward to us adopting her. Growing up, Ashley seemed to want to do her own thing. I tried getting her into sports like my boys, but she barely stuck to anything. She played Little League and soccer for only one year and then never tried sports again. Ashley didn't seem to like school much either, as she struggled through her school years. I wanted her to get a better education, so I sent her to Lexington Academy instead of Peabody High School. She attended Lexington Academy from ninth to twelfth grade. Even though she graduated, her senior year was her hardest because she got pregnant. Her pregnancy went well, and she had a beautiful baby girl named Calianna.

Charlotte and I wanted Ashley to be responsible, and we helped her to get back on her feet. Ashley started applying for jobs. Quite frankly, Ashley appeared lost and didn't know what she was going to do with herself. She would pick up odd jobs here and there. She tried working at small diners, one of them was D'Orsi's restaurant in Peabody. She tried working at a nursing home as a CNA. Ashley then decided she wanted to get her CDL license as a tractor-trailer driver. She went to school in Lexington to learn how to drove an eighteen-wheeler. She did well in school and passed the exam easily. She started driving all over the United States for a company and then she switched jobs and drove for a repo company. Ashley was dating a man named Jonathan for a while and got pregnant again. This time she had a handsome baby boy, who they named Cayden. Jonathan left Ashley to go to South Carolina, which is where he originally grew up, because his grandmother died. He decided to stay down there with his family after attending his grandmother's funeral. Ashley had to travel down south for her job and met up with Jonathan while she was down there. She liked it there and didn't want to come back home to Peabody. We often cared for Ashley's children while she was away. She wanted to stay down south to work things out with Jonathan. Since they reunited, they had their son, Cayden, move there with them. Jonathan was living with his family, so they all moved in there together. Ashley's daughter, Calianna, stayed in Massachusetts with her father's family because her father (Bryan) didn't want her to move. Jonathan and Ashley were having arguments, and she started spending more time with Jonathan's fraternal twin brother, Joseph. Well, it wasn't long before Ashley started to date Joseph. Ashley got pregnant with Joseph's child. She named her baby boy Zailian. Joseph thought it was only right to marry Ashley, so they got married by the justice of the peace.

Joseph and Ashley weren't too comfortable living there anymore with the family, especially because she was previously dating Joseph's brother. Ashley wanted to move back to Massachusetts, but they weren't prepared to get their own place at that time. They packed up and moved back here anyways. Charlotte wouldn't let Joseph move in with us because she was upset that Joseph didn't ask her for permission to marry her daughter. Joseph moved in with his uncle and Ashley and the two boys stayed with us. We weren't too happy with all of Ashley's choices and tried our best to get her back on track. Calianna stayed with us a few days a week, and the rest of the week she stayed with Bryan's family.

Approximately six months later, Ashley and Joseph got their own apartment in Peabody. Just the boys lived with them, and Calianna stayed with us and Bryan's family because Bryan didn't want his daughter to live with Joseph. Unfortunately, Ashley and Joseph could not stay in an apartment for a long period of time. They kept moving from one place to another because they had problems in every place they lived. They lived in Salem for a short period of time, and the children had to keep switching schools, which we didn't think was good for them. Bryan wanted Calianna to go to Lynn Public Schools, where he's from. Charlotte and I assisted with bringing Calianna to Lynn each morning when it was Ashley's custody during the first half of the week because Ashley was working. Joseph was working for hotels in Boston and driving the shuttles to the airports. Ashley would drive for different truck companies. She drove for a trash company for a while and then for Greyhound. I hoped that Ashley would stay with a job to get some stability in her life. Finally, Ashley found a job that I think she'll stay at for a while driving a bus for the MBTA in Boston. She got good pay and benefits, which would tremendously help her family. Hopefully, Ashley and Joseph will stop moving so much and settle down because they also lived at the Hampton Hotel. I want the children to stop bouncing around from place to place and finally have a place to call home. I have been stressed thinking about the children because they deserve better and should not be growing up like that. It seems as if they keep losing friends as soon as they meet them.

After the Leukemia surgery, I was out of work for about three months before I felt strong enough to go back. I was looking forward to seeing everyone again. They all welcomed me back with open arms. Some of the guys raised about $300 for me while I was out. Though I was feeling better, there were times when my hip would act up and the pain would linger for a while and affect my ability to walk and stand for long periods of time. I had a lot of work to do, and being on my feet all day became tiring. For quite some time, I had been considering retiring anyway. I had to retire even though I was only about fifty-two years old at the time. Working at the post office alone, I put in a good fifteen years of time, so I received forty percent disability.

Leon's son Robbie (left), Hector (center), who played Little League for Leon, and Leon (right)

Leon's adopted daughter, Ashley

Chapter 8

Retirement

It was nice having a break from working, but after a couple of months I wanted to do more, so I started to look for a part-time job. I liked working with children, so I applied for a job at the local schools for a substitute teacher position. Soon after putting in my application, I started receiving calls and filled in for teachers at various schools in the area. I started at the Higgins Jr. High School in Peabody. Unfortunately, the children there didn't seem interested in learning anything. They didn't behave too well either and were disrespectful. I was not going to tolerate that kind of behavior and was not willing to test my patience any longer. It was too bad because I loved to teach and coach. Two girls even started to fist fight in the back of my class one day. I broke up the fight right away by separating them from each other. I spoke to them outside of the classroom. The girls told me they'd been fighting for a long time, even outside of school. They lived in the same neighborhood and just didn't like each other. I couldn't understand why they could not get along or in the alternative mind their own business and ignore each other. They reminded me of the Hatfield-McCoy feud back in West Virginia. That family fought all the time to the point they were out of control in the neighborhood. After

I told the girls they needed to avoid each other, a hall monitor walked by and asked what was going on. I didn't want to see these two girls get into trouble with the principal, so I tried covering up for them, but the hall monitor wasn't hearing it and the girls ended up in the office.

I decided to try coaching one of the school teams. I was allowed to coach the boys basketball team. Some of the parents were just as bad as some of the students because they would come to me and tell me how lousy I was and that I shouldn't be coaching. I kept my cool and my patience throughout all of that, but I really didn't want to work for that school anymore. The faculty was great to me and the principal wanted me to teach full time, but I never took her up on her offer. I had to pass on that because my sanity was more important and there was too much drama.

One time when I was substituting, another teacher brought some shocking news to my attention. She told me she was reading a book called *Wayward Sheriffs of Witch County* by Bob Cahill and my name was in it. I couldn't believe it, and I had to go see it for myself. I went to the library after school to find the book. Sure enough, my name was right where she said it was. My full name and a complete description of me and my duties as a correction officer described to a T.

The school vice principal came to me one day and asked me if I could go on a field trip to monitor a boy who had emotional problems. I didn't mind volunteering at all. When I met the boy, he seemed very nice and polite. We went to Canobie Lake Park in Salem, NH, and had a nice day. He was very well behaved. The vice principal even gave me money to spend on the boy that day. Later I met his parents at a meeting I attended at Catholic Charities. It was for parents who adopted children. That was when I found out he was an adopted child. Unfortunately, he was lonely and didn't really have many friends. Then years later I heard he committed suicide after high school. What a shame. He was such a good young boy, only nineteen years old. His parents were heartbroken, and I wished there was something I could've done to save him from his plight.

I filled in at the Welch School but not for long because the children's behavior was the worst I've ever seen anywhere. Not one child would listen.

They were basically running amok. There were children screaming and running around everywhere with no order or discipline. Not one teacher could get a grip on these children, and neither could I. I didn't see how they could get an education at this school. They were disrespectful to all the teachers. I tried talking to one girl's mother because she was very disrespectful to me. Her mother started crying and apologizing and told me she couldn't control her daughter either. I couldn't believe this girl was disrespectful to her own mother. There wasn't any point of me being at this school, so I refused to go back. It wasn't long after I stopped working that I heard about a big investigation going on. I didn't get all the details but heard they were looking for a body that might have been buried there. They dug up that whole schoolyard, but as far as I know they didn't find anything. I was surprised to hear about something like that happening in our town. Peabody is a nice place to live and raise kids, at least that was what I believed.

I continued bouncing from school to school wherever they needed me. I didn't mind because I love meeting new people and children. I actually filled in for my wife a couple of times at Classical High School in Lynn. She was a distributed ED teacher and taught a computer class mainly, but also some typing and shorthand. All I could do was cover the class because I couldn't teach that kind of class because of the special education requirements. The students just worked on their own but had a lot of free time. They would ask me if they could leave and go to the bathroom or something and they wandered off sometimes and disappear for a while before they returned to class. Charlotte didn't like how I ran the class, but there really wasn't anything I could do with those students, so I didn't fill in anymore.

I substitute teaching at Lynn Tech a few times, which was a nice experience. The faculty was pleasant, and the students were well behaved. They were all there to learn a trade, so they were quite focused on their interests. Once I covered the auto body class, and I certainly couldn't teach that class because I was not experienced in it. The staff taught me how to teach a writing and English class, which made it easier for me to fill in for the teachers there. I volunteered to coach their basketball team because I liked the students and their eagerness to show their athletic talents. I got them in shape and had them go through some running drills. I'd teach them some fundamentals like block out, shoot layup, defense, rebounding, and discipline.

I worked at St. Mary's High School and often looked forward to them calling me to fill in there because the students were well behaved. They seemed to enjoy my presence. I enjoyed teaching children that were eager to learn. I love teaching religion and about the Bible, especially about Jesus. We studied the Old Testament, all about Sampson, Delilah, and Moses. The students thought it was funny when I told them how Delilah cut Sampson's hair and that he became weak from the cut. He eventually got his strength back from God, though. Then I taught some history on slavery and how Abraham Lincoln freed the slaves. He issued the Emancipation Proclamation on January 1, 1863, as the nation approached its third year of bloody civil war. The Proclamation declared "that all persons held as slaves" within the rebellious state "are, and hence forward shall be free." I coached for the baseball and football teams because I enjoyed teaching the children at St. Mary's. The freshmen football team never won a game until I coached them.

After some time, I was getting calls from Peabody High to fill in for their social studies teacher. One time the teacher left a test for me to give to the students. No one could concentrate, though, because the class next door was being extremely loud and unruly. The children were screaming and slamming doors. I went to see what was going on and couldn't believe what was happening in this classroom. The children were running around like it was a playground. At first, I didn't think there was a teacher in the room until I saw a gentleman sitting behind the teacher's desk with his feet up on the desk, acting nonchalant. He was also a substitute teacher, but I couldn't believe he would just sit there and let those children run loose like that. Someone had to intervene, so I told the children to sit down and be quiet because my students were taking a test. They all froze and looked at me with such surprise. Then they did as I told them. The teacher apologized to me as he abruptly removed his feet from the desktop. Mrs. Wilson, the principal from Higgins, called Peabody High School and told them she needed me at her school because the students listened to me the most. So, I worked at the Higgins School mainly for about another year.

One day during my time of substitute teaching, I decided to take a break to attend my son Henry's football game at East Stroudsburg University in Pennsylvania because it was his last year there. I took the $4,000 that I had in my retirement with the Peabody school system and left. I booked a hotel for eight weeks in Pennsylvania. While I was there, Angela, the owner of Boston Casting, called me for a casting job. She needed me to do a big, national commercial for her. I was going to pass it up because I planned on being in Pennsylvania for eight weeks, but she wouldn't take no for an answer. The company really wanted me. I came back for the shooting date, and they paid me $3,000, so it was well worth it. I wanted to do it for Angela because she was always good to me. It was a good year, and Henry was nominated for the top senior football player. He always tried his hardest and did well. Unfortunately, he didn't win the award he deserved, but it was nice that he got nominated.

Leon's students that he coached

Chapter 9

The Museum

One day I was walking by the Peabody Essex Museum and saw a security guard out front. I was curious about the museum, so I approached him to see if I could get some information. It sounded quite interesting, and I thought it might be nice to work at the museum part-time. I asked the guard who I should contact to apply for a position as a security officer. Once I applied, I was called in for an interview within a week. The supervisor hired me right away because of my strong background in the field. I was looking forward to my first day, but unfortunately it was quite boring. I was in charge of one of the gallery rooms, where I spent my whole shift in the same room. I was hoping for a position where I was more involved and would be able to move around more. I was on my feet all day like a statue. All I had to do was make sure everyone stayed quiet, especially when groups came in. I had to make sure no one touched anything, especially the children. The more I worked there, the more I began to like it. I got to meet new faces as time went on, and I enjoyed interacting with people. I worked more hours as time went on and made more money. When it was slow, I started reading the labels on the displays, which I enjoyed and absorbed quickly. Then I was able to teach and educate people as they toured the museum. Groups of people would come in from all over the world to tour our museum, which became quite popular over the years. This brought back memories of being a teacher again, which I loved. Everyone seemed to enjoy learning about the history of the museum. The Peabody Essex Museum is over 300 years old. It's been there since 1799. Surprisingly, even the children that come in on field trips were interested in the history.

    I worked in the Maritime Room at the museum for some time, which stands for The Body of Water. We had objects and artifacts from ships from the 1800s arriving at the museum. Many people wrote in about how they enjoyed talking to me and couldn't believe all the history I knew. Some of my coworkers got a little jealous, but I didn't mind because I enjoyed and appreciated people taking the time to write letters of appreciation to me. I enjoyed covering the room for the Yin Yu Tang Chinese House. It was very interesting, and I learned new information just as much as I enjoyed teaching it. I learned about a wealthy merchant, Huang, who built a stately sixteen-bedroom house in China's southeastern Huizhou region and called it the Yin Yu Tang House. It was built of timber frame construction with a tile roof and exterior masonry walls of sandstone and brick. The house had two reception areas, a storage room, and a courtyard in the center. Eight generations of the Huang family were able to call it home. In the mid 1980s, the house became empty for quite some time. The local and national authorities got permission from the owner's descendants for the house and its contents to be relocated to the Peabody Essex Museum in Salem, MA. I would talk about the Chinese Cultural Revolution. It was a sociopolitical movement in the People's Republic of China from 1966 until 1976. China's youth from the Red Guard groups are socialist groups around the country. They split into rival factions and at times carried out attacks in open battle. Mao Zedong was the communist leader in 1966. He started what became known as the Cultural Revolution and wanted to assert his authority over the Chinese government. Thousands of Chinese people would come from China to see this exhibit. Once a Chinese woman asked me if I was Chinese because I knew so much information. All I could do was laugh, and then said to her, "Do I look Chinese?"

The president of the museum and other staff members in charge were the ones who would research for more historical items to add to the museum. They would come in quite often to check on the museum and make changes. I got to know them pretty well and shared some of my background experience with them. They seemed quite interested because they told me I should write a book. I thought about it for a while and even talked to my family and friends about the idea, and they all encouraged me to write a book. I was still working a lot at the museum, though, and couldn't really look into it at the time. As much as I enjoyed working there, it was taking a toll on me from being on my feet all day. My hip would act up at times, which eventually caused pain in my back.

Due to the continuous pain in my hip when I walked, my doctor took x-rays and ran tests. I don't think it helped that I ignored the pain and tried to compensate by walking differently to feel better. The doctor scheduled my surgery right away before it got worse. That day, I told my supervisor about the surgery. It was decided that I would take a leave of absence for at least a couple of months. I had my surgery on April Fool's Day of 2019. After the surgery, I stayed in the hospital for one night. My doctor was going to let me stay another day, but I chose to go home. They sent me home with a walker later that day. It wasn't long before they got me in for physical therapy. I was mainly doing water exercises in the pool. After a couple of months, I returned to work like I told my supervisor I would. But it wasn't long before I decided to give my resignation notice because it wasn't that easy for me to stand all day anymore. My superior was surprised because he knew how much I loved learning the history of all the new artifacts and teaching it to the guests, plus after fifteen years working at the museum, he did not expect me to resign. On my last day I was assigned to work on the third floor, which was my favorite floor in the museum. The India gallery of contemporary art was on one side and the Japan gallery of contemporary art was on the other side. I loved the artwork, and the paintings were outstanding and breathtaking to the guests. The colors were so bright you could not miss them. There was a porcelain piece from Japan with red, blue, and green flowers and birds and dragons. It was detailed and looked real. There were paintings and items from the seventeenth and eighteenth centuries. Back then the captains of ships were called merchants, and they would be the ones trading the items to bring to the Salem museum and other historical places. A beautiful, unique, shiny maple wooden desk from the 1800s and made with stingray skin was also on display. A lot of people would walk by the displays without reading the information, and I would point out the history of the displays to them. As I began to lecture about the artwork, I noticed the guests would become more interested and ask me questions.

There were two paintings from the India contemporary art gallery—Rickshaw Man and Over the Bridge. Rickshaw Man was cubism, and the man in the painting looked deformed and resembled Frankenstein. His right hand had just four fingers. He had been pushing the rickshaw for many years. He may have started pulling a rickshaw at age eleven. He was pulling a beautiful Indian woman in the rickshaw. Her eyes showed sadness for the rickshaw man. The Over the Bridge painting displayed heartaches, sadness, and hopelessness. One man had bloodshot eyes. He had just left the village of pain. Another man had his arms around that man's neck, giving him support from the terror that he had seen in the village. The devil was lurking and making chaos in the village. One good thing about the painting was that it was very colorful and beautiful. Well before the end of my last shift, some of my coworkers came up to me to say goodbye and wished me luck. My supervisor invited me to come back for the employee Christmas party that year.

Finally, I made an appointment with my primary doctor, who I trusted like a brother. I always looked forward to seeing him because we always had great conversations and had a lot to share. I learned he had a band at one time and even played at the jail for inmates. He told me he enjoyed playing the piano. As he got to know me over the years, he wrote a song about me called "Soul Man." One day I was in a lot of pain when I went to see him. It was a steady and shooting pain going down the right side of my leg and foot. I ignored it for a long time, but it was causing me back pain. My doctor tried moving my leg and foot, but the pain was so bad that I instantly jumped.

Immediately, the doctor said, "I am going to make a referral for you to see a specialist at Mass General." When I saw the specialist, he knew the symptoms and reviewed my health before he required that I have back surgery.

It was nice to be home more often and have time to myself, but it felt different not working or having a routine. I was able to sleep later and relax more. It was great for my health to rest after all that I had been through. I wanted to enjoy retirement by focusing on taking care of my health and wellbeing. I saw my family more and enjoyed the time I spent with my grandchildren when they came over. There was plenty of things for them to do in my big yard. They ran around the yard and played on the swing set. They played basketball in the yard and swam in our above-ground pool surrounded by a long deck. We had a decent-size house, thirteen rooms in total.

Charlotte worked part-time, and I ran most of the errands and things around the house, including cooking, especially around the holidays where I was known for my family's sweet potato pies. There were plenty of things to do around the house to keep me busy, including yard work. Having thirteen rooms to manage while Charlotte was working kept me busy most of the time. Things would pile up, and I would slowly clean up the house throughout the days and years. We had to store our children's belongings at our house because they did not have enough space at their small apartments. A lot of things were stored in our garage to prevent clutter, and this was a very big project when the time came to clean it out. Over time, I was able to bag up unwanted clothes and things that were too old and donate them to different organizations, such as Good Will.

My favorite thing to do was play golf. Going golfing was my number-one hobby, but I could not find the time to play any golf because I had way too much work to do around the house. Still, I was grateful to find the few times I could go golfing when I was working at the museum. There was a tournament in Saugus at the Cedar Glen Golf Course, and I participated. We raised money for HAWC, a program for abused women and children. This event was big and important, and many times it was recorded or filmed. I was interviewed by the program, and I was thrilled to help raise approximately $600 for the HAWC because it was going to a good cause. I would try to make time to play golf even though it was a long drive to the location. I donated money I had to the Brotherhood Club in Lynn because they could not afford the upkeep the club needed. I helped put money toward the bathroom that was in dire need of repair. I purchased a new toilet and new vanity and had my plumber install it.

There was a fundraiser to raise money for the African American College Fund, which was held on the South Shore with James Kimball and Andre Tippett, a professional football player, who was the master of ceremonies. I participated in their tournament, and it cost me eighty dollars to play. This money went toward the fundraiser. There were times when I took a little vacation to play golf out of state, and it was great to enjoy a getaway. I visited my friend Ethal in San Diego. She was the president of the Paramount Golf Clubs and a hall of famer. She played professionally in a lot of tournaments. Sometimes Ethal came over to visit me in the summer, which was nice, but I preferred going to San Diego since the weather was beautiful and the golf courses were better than where I customarily played. Once in a while, I went to Reno to play a tournament at the Paramount Golf Clubs. There were more scratch golfers there, which meant they would shoot par games in two and three strokes. Other than that, I would practice and play for fun with my friends. We would play eighteen holes or practice at driving ranges. We played a lot of golf in Peabody at Peabody Meadows Golf.

Chapter 10

Memories

Over time I started to drift away into my past. I had flashbacks and memories of my childhood and family. I would think about the times when I took vacations and traveled to West Virginia by train. Family members and friends would organize reunions over the years. It was always a pleasure to see my family and to stay in touch. Every two to three years, we would get friends together at the Charleston Civic Center with at least 1,000 people who traveled from all over for the Simmons Reunion, named after the Simmons BLK School. I remember going to the reunions since the 1970s. As long as there were plenty of people attending, there would always be a reunion. The reunion kept us up-to-date and close to friends. Dressing up was one of the best parts of the reunion besides seeing the changing faces as we grew old. Men commonly wore suits and ties, and sometimes tuxedos. My father came to the reunion with me and my wife once. My father enjoyed attending the reunions because it was a way to interact and socialize with everyone. Exchanging stories about our past and present lives was interesting. My father sure enjoyed his scotch while socializing. His favorite scotch was Johnny Walker. I remember when I saw my neighbor Hazel, and we were both happy to see each other. She was more like a sister to me, and I could talk to her about anything. It was nice to reminisce about our past together. My old neighbor Otheletta Blake had fond memories to share. I was very close to her parents. Otheletta talked about her parents a lot. She adored them just as I did. Her mother was intelligent and was a sweetheart. Unfortunately, she had MLS and was wheelchair bound as long as I could remember. It was always a pleasure to see my neighbor Mrs. Holt. She used to be a schoolteacher in town. She was a sweet little lady. She was very kind to offer me chores or work around her house. Anytime I was given work to do in the neighborhood I would take it because it was a little extra cash in my pocket.

My friend Floyd Thomas was still in West Virginia when I came to visit. He was smart, a great football player, and a great student. For some reason the children called him termite. After he completed high school, he went to a tech school then went into the military. He became a firefighter and eventually moved to Columbus, Ohio. He loved riding his Harley Davidson motorcycle. I cannot think of anyone who loved motorcycles as much as Floyd. He traveled all over on his bike. Thinking back, I remember his dad umpired some of my baseball games when I was growing up. His dad was always a pleasure to be around. Floyd would attend the reunion and sometimes there would be a guest speaker. One of my friends, Sammy Carter, spoke one year. I was surprised to see him because he was in a wheelchair due to MS. It was hard to see Sammy in the wheelchair; he was great friend and a smart man who attended West Virginia State College before he joined the Army. Sammy became a colonel and had lots of experience and stories to share about his experience in the Army. He spoke highly of Simmons High School and the history about it. Sammy had a younger sister named Sissy who could sing. She was a majorette and taught baton and dancing at the high school. They would march down the streets in custom made costumes and do bunny hops. The bunny hops originally came out on the *Anthony Ray Show* in 1953. Sammy shared stories about his dad, Mr. Carter, who was generally friendly. He was the sheriff of Fayette and worked at a small, local liquor store. Sammy's mother, Mrs. Carter, was a schoolteacher at Simmons High. I was always happy to be in her presence. The whole family was nice.

Whenever I visited the Carters, a good friend named Billy Thomas was there. He was a kind man and a well-dressed gentleman. Billy was an excellent basketball player. He left high school when he attended Montgomery because his family moved to Chicago during the school year. Billy had a couple younger brothers named Gregory and Skitterbug. Both brothers were young and timid, and the children in the neighborhood would often tease them. Mrs. Thomas was protective over her sons, and she would get irate because the children would not stop teasing them. The brothers would keep to themselves when the children were playing outside. Billy continued with his love for basketball when he moved to Chicago and later played semi-pro basketball. Unfortunately, I learned Billy was gun downed and met an untimely death in the 1960s from a drive-by shooting while he was on his porch drinking lemonade. Billy was only sixty years old when he met his untimely death. I was shocked to learn about it because he had potential and was such a great friend. I sat and reminisce about the time he would sit on his front porch. I remember the fun times I had with Billy. He could run fast when he was chasing us around and managed to tickle us to make us laugh. His family had a rooster that would go crazy chasing us around the yard and jumping on top of our heads trying to peck at us. We often call Billy "Chicken Bill" because his rooster reminded us of the roosters in the movie *Roots* with the character they called "Chicken George." Billy would train his roosters to fight and kill for gambling. Whenever we played, Billy would chase us around, catch us, and put our heads between his legs and rub his knuckles real fast on the top of our heads.

I had so many good friends. I cannot forget about J.D. Martin. J.D. was short for James Davis. He grew up in Mount Place, which was located near our house. He had a brother named Alfred and a sister named Debbie. His mom treated me like a son. She didn't treat me any different from her own children. She always welcomed me into her home. J.D.'s dad was absent because he died at a young age in a freak accident. A train slammed into his car and he suffered pneumonia while in the hospital. I visited J.D. at times when I took the train back to West Virginia. Growing up, we all would play poker and black jack. He got married to a wonderful woman named Joan from Wells, England. J.D. moved to Washington, DC, and he and his wife had one son together. Out of all the reunions, J.D. came only once, and this surprised me because I had fun being around him. J.D. liven up the party and drank like a fish. I can still see him sporting a scotch in his hand, while he gazed over at Otheletta, his childhood crush. A short time after, I learned J.D's sister died of breast cancer in her thirties. When I visited J.D. in Washington, DC, it took about four hours by train and he would meet me and drive me to his home. I felt welcomed at J.D's home; he could cook well ,and he entertained me with his cooking skills. He made me big breakfasts. The time was spent well, being around J.D.; however, J.D. didn't take care of his health because he chained smoked and indulged in drinking alcohol more than the average person should, in my opinion. It was unfortunate because he was a good person. He suffered from kidney failure and was receiving dialysis treatment. His wife made a sacrifice to give him one of her kidneys, but the day the procedure was to take place, he ended up dying on the operating table. He was only in his fifties.

Someone approached me at one of the reunions, but the person was unrecognizable to me. It was Hazel, my old neighbor. I would normally have recognized her even though she was ten years older than me. She looked out for me as a child and the other children in the neighborhood. She was only a kid herself, but every child looked up to her like a big sister. One time, Hazel hit a boy named Bobby Joe, who was the singer for the Cool Cats Band. They were popular in the local clubs. Hazel struck him over the head with a pan because he picked on me all the time, and he would also pick on the other children. Bobby wasn't that bad because he behaved like the other teenagers in the neighborhood. Hazel's parents were Mr. and Mrs. Gay. Her mother was a homemaker and her dad worked at the coal mine. We called him Sug or Sugar because he was a sweet man who treated us with kindness. Hazel was usually good to me and looking out for my best interests, especially when she talked me out of joining the Marines, and I didn't waver from taking her advice to join the Air Force. After Hazel graduated, she became a nurse and worked at the Montgomery Hospital. She married at a young age to a man named Paul, who was a decent military man. He served in the Army. They had two lovely daughters. Paul and Hazel raised them to be productive in society. As unpredictable as life can be, Paul died in his sleep unexpectedly of a brain hemorrhage.

The reunions were something exciting every year, but not many schools continued to have reunions as frequent as ours. I think ours continued because of the large number of attendees. This could be because we were close in Montgomery. Mr. Collins, a teacher at Montgomery High School, should be given the credit because he started the reunion; he became great friends with my father during the time he kept the reunions organized and going every year. Mr. Collins kept it going as long as he could for a good thirty years starting in the 1970s. A few people helped with organizing the reunion, such as Mrs. Caroline Blackman. Mrs. Blackman was a volunteer secretary at the Simmons reunion held in Charleston. Her complexion was fair, and she had a son, Eddie Ferguson, who was one of my best friends growing up.

Orange Smith was also at this reunion. She was a fairly good friend who I dated in the past. She was a gorgeous woman. I requested to come over to her house one time. She lived about ten miles away from me, but I didn't mind walking miles to see a pretty woman. We would walk together in and around her neighborhood, which is as far as the relationship went because she told me she was not interested in dating, but we remained friends. She did, however, marry a friend of mine named Kenneth Hopkins. Kenneth and I played football together. He was a linebacker and won the "All Conference" award. I won the "All State All Mention Award." Kenneth went to college and became an engineer and worked for an oil company in Louisiana. Orange never continued her education after high school, but she was a great mother, raising the two children she and Kenneth had together. We kept in touch over the years and exchanged Christmas cards. We kept in touch through Facebook a lot since social media became more popular.

There were two brothers named Ray and Charles who were like cousins to me. They were older than me too. Grandma raised them and their two sisters, Chic and Barbara. Their mother died young and their father, Tom, married Grandma. Tom worked at the coal mine until he started his shipping business. Chic and Barbara left West Virginia and married young. Chic moved to Pittsburg, and Barbara moved to Sandusky, Ohio. After graduation, Charles moved to Washington, DC. Ray went into the Air Force for four years and became an engineer. He worked at G.E. in New Jersey and Chicago. He married a woman named Marge and had two boys. Ray and Charles attended the reunions, but the sisters never went. One of Charles's boys currently lives in Jersey, but unfortunately his other son died in a car accident. He slid off the road and slammed into a tree before the car flipped over.

Dwayne Sheppard attended the reunions. He was well known for his piano skills and voice. He sang a little for the Cool Cats. Dwayne knew how to play football, although I never got a chance to play with him. His family didn't live too far from us, they were just at the top of the hill of Mount Place, and his dad owned a restaurant and a small motel rooming house business. I used to go to the restaurant to enjoy one of their famous bologna sandwiches. Later, Dwayne became a police officer in Washington, DC, and he worked along with J.D.

The reunion was something I looked forward to because it was the opportunity to connect with the people I missed. The get-together with old friends and family to talk about old times was something to cherish in the moment for those who have gone on to the afterlife and those who were still around. It was my moment to tell everyone what was on my mind and what I had done with myself since high school as it pertains to my family and friends. Over the years I often wondered how people were doing. The reunion was something Mr. Collins created and made sure it was an everlasting memory that lasted for at least the weekend each time we met. The reunion was not cheap, which explains why some people did not attend. The cost of attending was not a problem to me because it was a once a year event. I would make it my duty to arrive Friday afternoon at the hotel and settle before I went to the lounge that evening. Not everyone came on

Friday; some people arrived on Saturday. But most came on Friday, and we would get together for social hours.

The big event on Saturday evening always included a big dinner and dance. On Sunday morning, we had brunch together and went to a big park for a picnic. By Sunday afternoon and evening, we would wrap up the reunion. Most people headed home, but I stayed a couple extra days. The next train out was Wednesday afternoon, so I got to rest after a long weekend and tour my old territory. I visited my best friend Johnny Webb and his family up in Beckley, which was about sixty miles from Montgomery. Johnny was a people person and got along with almost anyone. He was tall and played basketball like a pro. When we were in school, Johnny brought home As and Bs, unlike me who struggled to bring home even a C. He eventually became a teacher. He had a big family, two brothers and two sisters. One of his sister's name was Messerit, and she led the band at Simmons High. I was surprised that no one came to the reunion from Johnny's family. His father, Johnny Sr., and his wife, Dolly, were big-time gamblers. Dolly was pretty tough, and she took charge of things. She was the bookie while they were in the gambling room in their house. The police were aware of the illegal gambling and raided their house one time. People scattered everywhere like gunshots were firing just to leave with their money on the table when the cops showed up. Dolly, the no-nonsense woman, got angry with Mr. Webb. She boiled water and put something like Drano in it and threw it at him. As luck was on him that day, the water missed him. I never knew what he did to his wife to have her react with such extreme and to administer such cruel harm on her husband. I was on my best behavior from thereon. I'll never forget the time when we were younger and were playing cowboy and Indians, and poor Johnny got shot in the eye with a BB gun. His brother was playing around with the BB gun when he accidently shot him. BB guns are just as dangerous as real guns because Johnny went blind in one eye. I'm not sure what happened to Johnny and his family ever since they moved to Beckley, but I missed them for sure, especially Johnny. I lost contact with them, because I lived Massachusetts.

I traveled to West Virginia and ran into Milford Ellis who went to Simmons High School. He was a little older and was in a higher grade. He was on his way to the reunion. Since we both would travel to the reunion by train, we decided to meet up in Washington, DC, to travel the rest of the way together to the other reunions. Milford was also an excellent basketball player in high school. His mother, Mary, was the slowest driver around town. Sometimes the children called her Maryboo, and people also called her slow Mary. She would hold up traffic with her family in tow.

During one of my visits to the reunion, I made my way to visit Freddie Charles, who I was told was my godfather. He was always good to me, and he would give me moonshine. One day he took me to the Black cemetery to show me what happened to it. They removed all the bodies and moved them to the Meadow Haven Cemetery upon the mountainside, in the city of Oakhill. They just made one mass grave for all the bodies. Freddie asked me if I could do something about it after what they had done, and I didn't know if anything was possible to be done at that point. I wish I knew sooner because I could have stopped it.

I often think back on my trials and tribulation wondering whether they began in Montgomery, West Virginia, or when I left to find my own independence. The same train that my mother took when she left Virginia to the East toward Newark, New Jersey, was the same train I took when I left. I found that I shared the same journey my father took when he came back without my mother and when I came back to visit. Between my father putting a 38-pistol to my head, my mother suffering with mental illness, people rioting and hurting each other and vandalizing properties, I became a stronger person due to my faith. In Jesus Christ I trust and pray as my protector and savior when the walls around me seem to be closing in. The aura of Jesus I felt when I heard unpleasant news was like a wind blowing through the trees on the mountainside, cooling down the hot hemisphere. The breeze that blows across the Kanawha River in West Virginia as the water moves rapidly down the stream brings a disturbed soul into a calming spirit. To experience such a warm feeling is knowing that a force is out there protecting me everywhere I go, all the way from the South China Sea to the Atlantic Ocean. With all these loving feelings, it helped me through my hardships of dealing with cancer, hate, and not being loved, but knowing my God loves me and watches over me like a guarding sparrow.

Where my life began was across the Kanawha River, and often I found myself going back to where I was born and raised. I traveled across the bridge over the Kanawha River each time I went to my high school reunion. Each time I went to my reunion, my class size became smaller and smaller because many have passed on. When I passed over the bridge, I saw the white cemetery untouched, and only the remnants of the Black cemetery that was there no more because it was replaced by a round-about. In the middle of the cemetery stood an old church, but what was left of the building was a few pieces of bricks and the frail stairway leading to the church. Driving over the Kanawha River brought back early recollections of my past, and the memories brought me to tears for the forgotten and those who have died.

Mrs. Jackson (left) and Mrs. Bego (right) at the Simmons reunion

Mrs. Holt (left) and Leon (right) at the Simmons reunion

Dewayne Sheppard at the Simmons reunion

Memories

Leon and friends at the Simmons reunion around early 1970s

Ray Gunn and his wife, Marge, at the Simmons reunion

Mr. Carter, guest speaker at the Simmons reunion

Leon (left), Alfred (middle), and Roy (right)

Debbie (Alfred's sister) sitting on the stairs.

Leon (right) going up the hill with Debbie (left).

Memories

Leon in his sheriff uniform

The dry cleaners where Leon worked

Leon's neighbor, Mrs. Fannie Ragland, at age 73. Photo taken on May 9, 1974.

The Tears That Flow Into The Kanawha River

Leon's neighbor Mrs. Broadnecks, who married Mr. Eugene Taylor. They were ages 68 and 69, respectively, when the photo was taken on May 9, 1974.

Leon (standing) and his neighbor Lanny Braxton

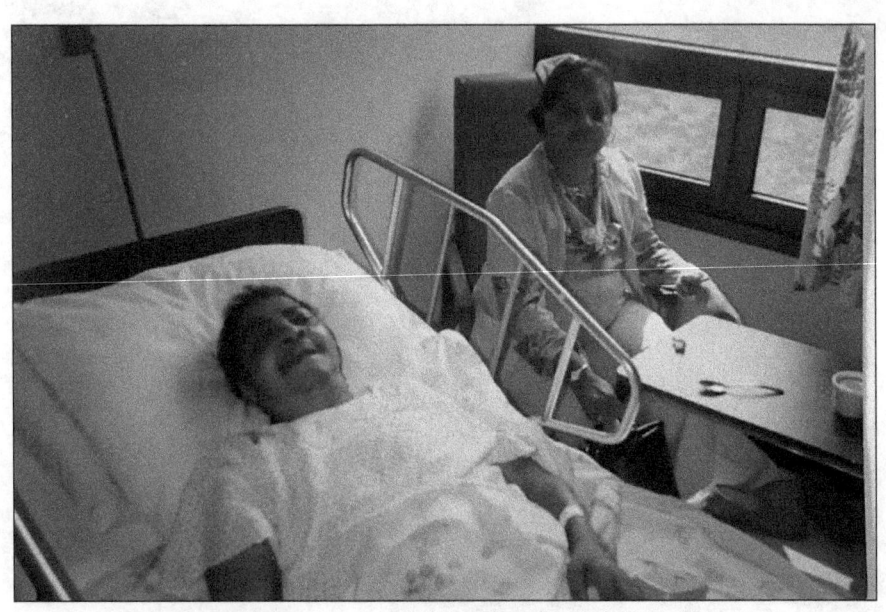

Leon's neighbor Mrs. Gay (who is Hazel's mother) and Leon's mother visiting her in the nursing home.

Memories

Leon's neighbor Mrs. Snyder and her husband

Roy (left) and Leon's cousins at the Breckenridge reunion

Leon's grandmother, Mary-Lou (second left), with stepdaughters at the Oakley's Easter celebration

THE TEARS THAT FLOW INTO THE KANAWHA RIVER

Roy and Rose (Leon's sister) at Marblehead Beach, Massachusetts

Leon's father and his girlfriend, Helen

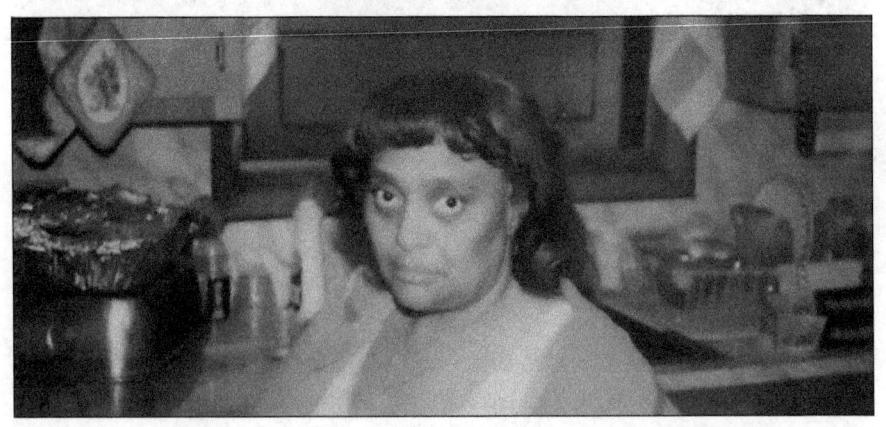

Leon's aunt Gertrude

Memories

Leon's great aunt Mamie

Betty Kite (right) and Leon's oldest sister, Lori

Leon's grandfather, Henry Sr. (right)

*Leon's father and his girlfriend, Helen
(left) and friends at a picnic*

Leon and Helen

*Mr. and Mrs. Collins
(Leon's father's best friends)*

Memories

Roy (left), Daniel, Leon's youngest son (center), and Leon (right)

Leon (right) and his wife, Charlotte, celebrating the award ceremony for then–Massachusetts Associate Attorney General Wayne Budd (left) with his wife

Men sitting at the railroad tracks in Montgomery, West Virginia.

The Tears That Flow Into The Kanawha River

In Montgomery, West Virginia, women ate Niagara Starch when they were pregnant and would develop blood level problems.

Leon's grandmother's house

Leon Breckenridge driving over the Montgomery Bridge by the Kanawha River toward the city of Montgomery, West Virginia. (Photo taken 9/6/2011).

Meadow Haven

On this site rests the forgotten souls of Montgomery West Virginians, mostly slaves and the families of the African Americans who made this their home. The only markers for their final resting place were stones placed on gravesites, only known to close family and friends. Let this memorial be a constant reminder of the sacrifice and never-ending courage of the true spirit of Montgomery, West Virginia. Now a poem in remembrance of the never again forgotten, as they made this their home with freedom.

> *The mountain forest is like a gate that protects the spirit of the forgotten people whose spirits live on …*
>
> *Their spirits sing in the rivers that flow slowly down the mountainside, and that is where they embrace each other once again.*
>
> By Leon Breckenridge

CPSIA information can be obtained
at www.ICGtesting.com
Printed in the USA
BVHW081608260521
608179BV00005B/1145

9 781662 813160